TIGER FIST

TWO STORIES

Nnamdi Carew

A Novella

Edited by
Winston Forde

Sierra Leonean Writers Series

TIGER FIST
Two Stories

Copyright © 2013 by Nnamdi Carew

ISBN: 978-99910-54-56-8

Sierra Leonean Writers Series

Warima / Freetown / Accra
120 Kissy Road, Freetown, Sierra Leone
Publisher: Prof. Osman Sankoh (Mallam O.)
publisher@sl-writers-series.org

ACKNOWLEDGEMENTS

I would like to thank all those who played a part in making my dream of becoming an author become a reality.

My Almighty God and Creator

My parents Dr and Mrs Kojo Carew

My siblings Dr. Melvin Carew, Dr Melbourne Carew and Dr Louise Carew and Amani Carew

My grandparents, Mr. and Mrs. Ade Palmer, and Mr. Francis Carew

My Editor, Mr. Winston Forde (Uncle Coolie)

Prof. Osman Sankoh and all the team of Sierra Leonean Writers Series (SLWS)

My Principal, (Madam J. Davies), teachers and classmates of The Apex International School, Freetown, Sierra Leone

I would like to specially acknowledge my little brother Amani Carew (12years old) for drawing the cover photo of this book.

Jermaine Nnamdi Carew

The Hero's Awakening

Summary

Born with the potential to be the strongest and fastest creature to ever walk the Earth, Daniel Washington struggles with the popularity and wealth of his foster father and with the anger that hides a dangerous monster. Five years later, life becomes difficult as Daniel faces his teen problems. When an enemy of his past emerges, Daniel must control himself and know about the monster in him.

Chapter 1

How it All Began

There was once a scientist named Austin Blake, who spent much time learning about legendary beings that had existed before the human race. He had a wife named Bianca, and she was as determined as Austin to find some clear evidence that these alien creatures ever existed.

Many people mocked their great determination, and believed that these 'fantastic creatures' were nothing more than a myth. Austin and Bianca ignored everything being said about them, and continued their work to find out about these creatures. They both knew that such research would take great patience, and a lot of work for them to succeed.

Well, after five years, Austin and Bianca found a fossil of one of the three legendary beings. Austin knew that the fossil belonged to an Anabulaen, a great creature or being believed to be an ancestor of a wolf. Anabulaens were very common in that era of the legendary beings.

Austin, therefore, decided to continue to search for evidence of the other two legendary beings known as Tigerton and Tauren. The 'tigerton' is the mysterious hybrid of a tiger and a human being whereas the 'tauren' is a close cousin of a Minotaur, a creature who was half man, and half bull. Austin took Bianca, who at that time was six months pregnant, with him on his journey abroad.

They travelled to China where another of these creatures once lived.

A few months later, Bianca gave birth to a baby boy. The baby placed a smile upon the faces of his two parents, and they were very happy. However, neither Austin nor Bianca could think of a suitable name for their new baby.

But, they soon forgot their problem in their excitement from being very close to finding any tangible evidence of a Tigerton. What made this creature very unique is that it could live for thousands of years, and may still be alive even to this day.

One day, Austin went deep into the jungle, hoping to find traces of a Tigerton. He suddenly came to a halt shaking with fright. He had seen a giant paw print in the mud, but that was not entirely the reason why he was afraid. Right in front of him stood a giant creature with all the traits of a tiger, but it had the body structure of a very muscular human being.

Austin began to run as fast as he could, but he knew he didn't have the slightest chance of escaping. He also knew the creature to be, without any doubt, a Tigerton. To his relief, Austin caught sight of his house. He started shouting for help, but the Tigerton finally grabbed hold of him, and prepared to make a kill.

Bianca heard her husband's cry, and immediately rushed to the door. She shrieked in despair as she saw Austin lying dead by the porch with his whole body drenched in blood. She then saw the Tigerton, walking menacingly towards her. Bianca turned stiff with fright. The Tigerton wasted no time killing her in cold-blood.

Suddenly, a loud wail came from the house. The Tigerton had found Bianca's baby using its strong sense of smell, and acute hearing. The violent creature was just about to slaughter its prey when the helpless baby stopped crying, picked up a nearby pebble, and threw it at the Tigerton.

The creature realized that the baby wasn't really afraid of it. So the Tigerton refused to kill the baby, but instead placed its paw over him and murmured an incantation. Then the strangest thing happened. The baby's tan-coloured skin began to grow an orange fur, then a striped tail sprouted, and his teeth   turned into greatly enlarged canines.

The baby now looked like a tigerton cub. The Tigerton smiled and began to play with the cub until the cub transformed back into a human baby. The Tigerton then left the baby staring over his parent's bodies, with its blue eyes turning yellowish green.

About five minutes later, a young Chinese monk entered the blood-stained house. He had heard the cries for help, and followed the frantic sound, which led him to the house. However, he had arrived too late. He saw the bodies of Austin and Bianca, and suddenly heard a baby crying. He entered a nearby room, and found Bianca's baby playing with a ball of yarn on the floor.

Feeling sorry for the baby, the monk decided to take him to the temple, where he lived. At the temple, he told the other monks everything that he had seen. He decided to adopt the baby, even though he had discovered it to be a hybrid of human and tiger, a Tigerton, and named him Daniel.

Chapter 2

The Awakening of the Powers Within

Daniel grew into a kind, brave and a bit aggressive toddler. Even in his human form, his tigerton nature affected him. He was stronger than a young male elephant, and could run faster than a cheetah. This made most of the monks terrified of him. As a student of kung-fu, karate and shaolin, he was a dangerous opponent, leaving much body pain in his fellow students.

Despite this, he was his teacher's favourite. As a monk-in-training, Daniel learned how to be calm in any situation. He would spend most of his time running through the forest at such a fast speed that the human eye could not see his form. Thanks to his kindness, he had a lot of friends who were older than him.

One day, Daniel went into the forest with a few of his friends to gather some fruits, and herbs.

"Hey, guys. I'll race you up that hill." said the energetic Daniel.

"But we already know that you are the fastest among us." grumbled his friend Chan.

"Well, it is worth trying" teased Daniel, with a chuckle."Come on. I will go easy on you!"

"Hmph! Alright, Daniel" said Chun, Chan's twin brother. "I will play your game of speed."

And so the three boys ran off as fast as they could towards the hill. Once out of sight, a tall and muscular man came out of the bush with a pistol in his hand.

"All clear, boys!" he shouted.

Soon fifteen men armed with guns appeared from the bushes. This was the infamous 'forest dragon' Triad.

"Mr Lu Xing, where do you think the forest temple is?" asked one member of the triad.

"It should be straight up this path." Lu Xing replied."Soon I will make that old monk pay for what he did to my brother!"

Soon the forest dragon triad found the temple. With Xing's signal, they attacked the temple and everyone in it. Each martial artist and monk found it difficult to fight any of the well-armed triad. However, the elder monk, who is Daniel's adopted father and the accused killer of Xing's brother, remained as calm as a monk can be.

Meanwhile, high up on the hill, Daniel and his friends, Chan and Chun, filled their baskets with apples, peaches, bananas, and some burdock shrubs. Suddenly, Daniel stopped picking fruits and started to sniff. Chan soon realized this.

"What is it, Daniel?" he asked waving his hand towards Daniel's face.

"Quiet!" shouted Daniel."Listen. Do you hear that, or smell something?"

"I cann't smell anything." replied Chan.

"Don't mind him, brother." said Chun, humorously. "Dan must have wax in his ears."

"QUIET!" shouted Daniel, and his voice shook the hill on which they were standing. Daniel began to inhale deeply, ignoring his friends' speechless state.

"It is coming from the temple!" he exclaimed. "Quick! Let us head back!"

Before anyone could stop him, Daniel ran down the hill with overwhelming speed. Chan and Chun stood with their mouths wide open. They ran after him once they recovered from their shock.

Daniel reached the temple within seconds. He saw the monks in grave danger. Lu Xing caught sight of the young boy as he held a pistol at the old monk.

"Well, what a good-looking young-" began Lu Xing. But, the monk easily disarmed him by twisting his hand bearing the gun, forcing Lu Xing to release the weapon. A finger jab to the neck followed, easily rendering Lu Xing unconscious.

"Don't be threatened by their weapons!" shouted the elder monk."Don't forget your training. Take care of these fools quickly! And I'll get back to my meditation."

And so the monks of the temple started fighting back together with Daniel. According to Lu Xing, Daniel was doing a better job at defending the temple than any of his teachers and monks.

"Men! Time for phase two!" shouted Lu Xing, regaining full consciousness. Soon more triad members arrived, outnumbering the monks. Despite the odds, Daniel continued to outwit each thug he faced.

"This boy! He is like a pest!" said Lu Xing, angrily. "It would be better when he is out of the way!"

He then raised his pistol at Daniel who quickly sensed what was about to happen. Bang! A bullet was fired. Daniel was about to manoeuvre the bullet but was violently pushed aside by the elder monk. Without looking at him, Daniel knew that the elder monk was shot. Lu Xing laughed wickedly.

"This is better than I imagined!" smirked Lu Xing. "I even had my vengeance that I promised."

Daniel became very angry. His fist clenched, his muscles bulged and his eyes glowed red.

Chapter 3

Unfortunate Events

Daniel tapped into the dormant powers his anger provided. His canines increased in length, he began to grow brown fur, and black stripes. Lu Xing began to tremble. The monks looked on in horror.

"He is a----" began Lu Xing. He then droped the gun with fright.

"A Tigerton?" asked a monk. Daniel turned into a giant, muscular, tiger-like creature. He roared with rage.

"Retreat!" shouted Lu Xing.

Before he could even move, Daniel gave him a powerful swipe, killing Lu Xing in the process. The panic-stricken triads started shooting at Daniel. To everyone's shock, Daniel was not affected by bullets. At amazing speed and strength one can hardly imagine, Daniel sent the triads flying out of the temple.

Despite the triads' defeat, Daniel started to destroy the temple, crippling the monks along the way.

"Daniel cannot control his rage as a Tigerton." exclaimed a healer. "He can destroy the whole jungle if he wants to!" "We are talking about a legendary monster, not a little boy anymore!" shouted a martial artist named Lao.

Meanwhile, Chan and Chun finally came down the hill, panting. They were so shocked to see a Tigerton on a rampage, instantly bringing the temple to the ground.

"STOP, DANIEL!!" shouted the elder monk, who was struggling on his last thread of life and was losing blood fast. Daniel grabbed the dying monk by the throat.

"You need to... control yourself, Daniel." said the choking monk."Do not... let your anger lead... you to destruction."

Daniel snarled at the monk but he suddenly had a flashback of how the monk cared for him ever since he was a baby. He loosened his grip on the elder monk who had taken care of him all his life. He soon realized what he had almost done: hurt his friends. During his sense of realization, Daniel had noticeably shrunk down to a less terrifying size.

Now, Daniel was a Tigerton who had successfully controlled his anger. He then rushed to the elder monk's side.

"Master, forgive Me." said Daniel in a deep, gruff voice. The monk looked at him with surprise.
   "Daniel, I am going to die soon." gasped the dying monk." Just know you are like a son to me."

"Master, what am I?" asked Daniel, looking at his big paws."I am like sort of a beast-"

"But you didn't let your rage destroy us." gasped the elder monk."It is rare for a Tigerton to control itself. But now, I have to leave you alone in this world."

"No. I still have much to learn from you." said Daniel, tears flowing down his face.

"Daniel, it is believed in the legendary scrolls of the Ancients that the most powerful Tigerton that ever existed would rise" gasped the monk, but he stopped as his heartbeat started to drop. Daniel looked at the hole in the old monk's chest and cautiously took the bullet with the tip of his claws from the monk's chest.

"Feeling any better?" Daniel asked, as he crushed the bullet into dust with his bare hands.

"Yes, but the time has now come for me to die" whispered the elder monk."Farewell, Daniel."

Daniel wiped his eyes as his adopted father died in his arms. He then slowly turned back into a human. All the monks mourned with Daniel as they buried the monk whose real name was Hung Li Chung, the following day.

The other monks told Daniel that he was the prophesied Tigerton. They also told him about Amaeron, the most powerful Tigerton to ever walk the earth and that by chance, he was the one who transformed Daniel into a Tigerton. Daniel found it very difficult to believe. A monk told him that was because he was a toddler and needed to age more to start his new life.

Daniel was given special training on kung-fu and karate for five years. He learnt how to master his super strength and super speed as a human. However, he was still very competitive and impulsive. He was very courageous and intelligent. The time came for him to leave China and travel to America, where he would find the answer to his past.

Daniel said goodbye to Chun, Chan and all of the other monks that he knew, and started off on his journey. He decided to run at a rate no human eye could see. In fact he was running so fast, he saw the tall trees and bushes as only a flash of green. The path became difficult to see due to his extremely fast speed. He soon left the jungle and, with a simple leap, jumped over the Great Wall of China.

He looked back in surprise.

"Great! Now I am the first human to actually jump over the Wall of China" he said to himself, sarcastically. He then continued running. Within two minutes, he ran across Tibet, India, and Persia and stopped in Turkey to ask for directions. Thanks to his Tigerton and Austin genes, he was quick to speak and understand other languages; in this case, Turkish. After asking for directions, Daniel continued running at supersonic speed, passing through countries within minutes.

Suddenly, he tripped over a rock and started tumbling in hyper speed fashion. After many bumps and hits on the rough ground, Daniel found himself face down on a perfectly tarred road. In a nick of time, he maneuvered a speeding taxi, landing on the pavement with people simply walking by, minding their own business. After brushing himself up, Daniel took a good look around.

Just then, the sound of a giant bell from above clanged in Daniel's ears. He looked up only to discover a giant clock tower that could be seen from a mile away.

A wide river flowed sluggishly along the massive building with the clock tower, and Daniel could see an impressive bridge downstream that looked like it could never fall. This made him wonder why the rhyme 'London Bridge Is Falling Down' was made.

"Excuse me," Daniel asked a red-haired girl, not much older than he was. "What is so important about this clock tower? Wouldn't it be simpler to carry a watch around?"

The girl didn't seem too interested in talking to a boy whose looks and accent suggested that he wasn't local.

"Well, why don't you get yourself a watch? From the sound of it, Big Ben 'ere isn't good enough for you."

Daniel seemed surprised when he heard this. "So this is the famous Big Ben the monks were talking about. So, does that mean I'm in London, England?"

"Well, you wouldn't find ole Big Ben in France now, would you?" The girl tapped her foot impatiently. "Do you have any more questions that don't need an answer, mate?"

"As a matter of fact, I have another question," Daniel said, misunderstanding the girl's mood. "How can I get from here to the United States of America?"

At this point, the red-haired girl had lost it. "Go suck a lemon, idiot! You'd either clear off or you wait till the police get 'ere!"

As the girl stormed off, Daniel sighed as he wandered to the bridge.

Suddenly, an alarm sounded from a nearby bank. A band of thugs carrying large sacks rushed out and got into a car. They started speeding away through the street.

Daniel became quite furious, but quickly controlled himself. He then decided to stop the thieves as a Tigerton, instead of being angry, and started transforming. He grew into a Tigerton faster than ever before. Due to his many years of training, Daniel gained the potential of obtaining limitless strength at will, thanks to his determination.

Meanwhile, the thieves were talking about how everything went according to plan. Suddenly, the car came to a screeching halt.

"What happens now, Roger?" asked Butch, the leader of the thieves.
"I- I don't know." stammered Roger. Suddenly, the car rose high above the ground. The thieves started to tremble.

"Wait a minute" said Butch as he looked over the window. He saw Daniel, lifting the car with one paw. People nearby looked at the creature in both awe and horror.

Before Butch could do anything ugly, Daniel gave a kick to his forehead.

Daniel then gave a mighty leap, still holding the car with his paw. The thieves began to scream as they soared higher into the air. Daniel landed on a high building and dropped the car on the roof.

"Get out of the car!" shouted Daniel. The thieves quickly got out of the car and each drew out a pistol.

"Alright, you freak!" said Roger."I don't know why you ruined our plans but you are going to fix everything, or you die!"

Daniel gave a yawn. The yawn was like a lion's roar to the thieves.

"Go ahead. Shoot me." replied Daniel as he sat licking his paw. The gang started shooting at their intruder without hesitation. They soon realised that the bullets only bounced off Daniel's body as if he was a rock. Each thief started to tremble and both panicked. They had never encountered a half-tiger, and half-human before on whom their bullets had no effect.

"Are you finished?" asked Daniel giving another yawn that nearly made Roger faint.

"We give up!" exclaimed a thief named Charles."We only ask for your name."

Daniel thought for a moment. What would be a name that would strike fear into the hearts of these evil souls?

A name to be given to a Tigerton with powerful fists.

"I am Tiger Fist!" he said and he gave a roar of triumph for a job well done.

He took the thieves to the nearest police station. He also then returned the stolen money to the bank. Town folks were unsure whether to cheer or scream at the fearsome creature.

A little boy bravely walked to Tiger Fist and thanked him for catching the thieves and returning the money to the bank.

"You're welcome, kid!" answered Tiger Fist in a deep, cheerful voice."My name is Tiger Fist"

The boy shook the giant paw of Tiger Fist. People around were more than convinced that the giant creature was indeed a lot kinder than it looked. Before he could leave, the people gave him several rounds of applause.

Having found a quiet place to sleep for the night, Tiger Fist transformed back into Daniel.

Chapter 4

The Beginning of a Life of Wealth

The next day, Daniel was given a meal by a kind chef, who had seen him helping disabled people to walk across the street. Daniel told the chef about his journey, and asked for directions. The chef didn't really believe how fast he could run but he was surprised to hear that Daniel was the son of Austin and Bianca Blake.

"*The* Austin Blake?" The chef asked doubtfully. "The man who discovered the skull of a beast called the Anabulaen?"

"He died nine years ago." Daniel replied, feeling rather amazed by his father's fame in England." I need to go to the United States to find a man named John Washington. I was told that he would know about my parents."

"Well, you asked the right person." said the chef with a grin."I just happen to be one of the chefs and a childhood friend of John."

"Could you tell me where I could run from here?" asked Daniel.

"W-Wait a second! Were you really serious about running to the United States?" asked the chef, who looked as if he was talking to a mad boy. Daniel was stunned by the question. After all, he was never doubted for his speed.

"Yes. Why?" asked Daniel. The chef didn't know whether to laugh and assume it was a joke or explain to Daniel the absolute nonsense he was saying. He decided to explain.

"Look, it is impossible for a man to run from here to Washington" he continued, sternly.

"I am not an ordinary boy, and that is what makes me special" said Daniel, proudly. Before the chef could say anything, the CNN reporter, Isha Sesay started to say something on TV that left the chef speechless and Daniel with a grin.

"Yesterday, in Turkey, a young journalist witnessed a young boy, possibly American running at supersonic speed. He even recorded the event, as the boy asked for directions from a local farmer."

And then a recorded video showed Daniel running so fast that he was almost a blur on the recorder.

"Whoa! Did you see that?" asked Ben Thompson, the journalist.

"Yes. It's all on the tape." said the photographer. The camera was turned to Ben for him to reply.

"Yes, this is the most amazing thing since the Great Wall of China. It is simply impossible for a boy or anyone to run at this speed." said Ben."He left a trail of dust behind like a truck in the desert."

"Now do you believe me?" asked Daniel, who started laughing at the chef's dumb-stricken face.

"I-I" began the chef, still not believing what he had just seen.

"Are you now going to give me directions?" asked Daniel. He then accidentally bent the metal spoon. The chef was as white as snow when he saw this. Daniel apologized and easily fixed the metal spoon.

"This is insane!" exclaimed the chef. "This is like a stupid dream!"

"Hello? Direction pleeease" said Daniel, cheekily.

"Don't do that ever again." warned the chef.

"What?" Daniel asked.

"Ask for directions in that cheeky tone" replied the chef."I insist that we take a plane to the U.S." carrying large sacks

"Did you say we?" asked Daniel, with astonishment.

"Yes. I have enough money to make the trip, and spend a year in that country" boasted the chef.

"I forgot to ask, but what's your name?" asked Daniel.

"My name is Greg Turner." replied the chef. "I am a personal friend of both John Washington, and your father."

"When is our flight?" asked Daniel, impatiently.

"I'll book us on the 12:15 flight." replied Greg, holding up the cell phone.

"Do you have any work for me to do?" asked Daniel, looking around the restaurant."I'll get this place ready for business in no time."

"Well, here is a list of things to do." replied Greg, handing over a large sheet of paper with tasks written on it.

"No problem, sir." said Daniel. He started walking away, but then stopped to ask how long it would take a human to do this work.

"Well, that's about forty-five minutes" answered Greg without asking why.

"Let me put that to the test." said Daniel with a grin, and with a whoosh of speed, he went to work.

Greg stopped to look at Daniel and was so shocked at his speed he didn't notice his chef's garb drop to the ground.

Daniel mopped the floor, dusted the tables and chairs, cleaned the windows and washed the dishes in exactly five minutes or perhaps less. Greg thought this was the craziest dream he'd ever had, or was it?

"Done!" said Daniel and watched Greg, recovering from his shock."So when do we leave?"

Three hours later, Daniel and Greg boarded an American Airlines flight for the United States. During the flight, Daniel received more information about his father and John Washington. Daniel had never felt so inactive and bored in his life.

When the plane landed in San Francisco, Daniel started stretching and exercising for a bit. John Washington and his butler, James Holland were waiting for them outside the airport. John was so anxious to meet Daniel.

"So, you're Daniel Blake." said John, looking at the young boy."You have your mother's eyes and your father's cheerful looks."

"Um, thank you very much." replied Daniel. He was lifting two heavy suitcases.

"Please allow me, young man." James pleaded.

Daniel simply gave the suit cases to James, who found it impossible to carry both of the suitcases at once. To boast his unnatural strength, Daniel balanced the suitcases on the tip of both index fingers like basketballs and started spinning them. This left John dumb-struck and James stuttering. Daniel then placed the suitcase on a trolley.

"Quite a strong fellow you are" John said, as they went toward his limousine. They had a long conversation.

"What was my father like?" asked Daniel to John.

"Well, he was friendly, determined and a man who won't stop to achieve his dreams" replied John.

"I remember the last thing he said to me was that I was his most prized and greatest discovery" said Daniel, his mind lost in memories."Then a monster such as I am now killed them for no reason."He couldn't finish the sentence because he was crying.

"Don't cry, tiger." said John, thumping Daniel on the back."You have to be brave when things are bad for you even at a time like this."

"How can I be brave when my life has been torn to shreds?" asked Daniel, wiping his tears.

"It doesn't matter now" said John, handing Daniel a packet of tissues."In life, we must move from the past. That is why I am going to adopt you, and you will live with me."

"Really?" asked Daniel as if he was asked to spend one million dollars.

"Of course I wouldn't let the son of a dear friend live on the streets" John replied. This made Daniel excited. When they arrived at John's mansion, Daniel began to look around. He was in heaven on earth.

"Which way is the gym?" asked Daniel looking at the chandeliers in the living room.

"Down in the basement...." began John, but Daniel was already in the basement working out.

It took John an hour to join Daniel. He found him working with 10 tonne weights, and running on a treadmill at 35 miles per hour. This left John speechless.

Soon, Daniel stopped to take a short break and noticed John. He had debated whether to tell him about his Tigerton powers or not, and concluded that he should.

"Um, sir?" he began. He then realized that John was still in his state of disbelief. "Uh, sir?"

"Yes, what is it?" asked John, finally recovering from his shock.

"I think I have to tell you something that is not going to be easy to explain." Daniel said. "You see, I am a Tigerton."

"What's a Tigerton?" asked John, scratching his head.

"It's a legendary creature that my dad was searching for at the time." Daniel replied. "He found it one day and it killed him along with my mother. When it saw me, its eyes glowed in mine."

"Interesting." Said John, sitting near Daniel." So, it left you unharmed."

"Not only that, it somehow gave me it's powers." Daniel said. "Do you want me to show you?"

"Alright, release the beast." John said without a second thought. Daniel began to recall the pain which he received from his foster father, Hung Li Chung who was killed by Lu Xing. His muscles started to bulge, his canines grew, and orange fur began to grow from every part of his body as he began to resemble a tiger. John became increasingly frightened as he watched the transformation.

"Well, how do I look?" Daniel asked in the deep gruff voice of a Tigerton. He started wagging his long striped tail. John now believed that this was one big dream. He sat down and wiped his eyebrow with a handkerchief.

"I know. This is how a Tigerton looks like." said Daniel, showing off his enormous muscles.

After John recovered from his shock, Daniel explained the case properly to him.

"The question is, why didn't that beast kill you?" asked John, while Daniel was lifting 30 tonnes of weight like a baseball.

"I don't know." Daniel said. "I cannot remember."

"Well, what matters most is that you're still alive." John said, tapping Daniel's fur.

"I need to find the answers to this." Daniel said, getting up from the floor."I will start by stopping crime in this state."

"No! You can't just roam the street facing thugs for no reason." John said.

"I have to make use of this." Daniel insisted. "Besides, bullets or knives cannot even haze me."

"I don't care!" shouted John. "You will only put your life at risk." This made Daniel growl violently and John jumped back with fright. However, Daniel controlled himself.

"Remind me never to make you mad." added John.

So Daniel enjoyed the life of wealth. John became his new foster father. Daniel's fortune changed over the years, and when the world realized that he was the son of Austin and Bianca Blake, he became very famous.

Five years later, Daniel grew into a stylish young teenager. He developed a liking towards tigers. He attended the Orange Stars High School. He befriended a school trickster named Alfred King who was about the same height, and of Mexican descent. Like Daniel, Alfred had a deep voice, and was very energetic. However, Alfred was regarded as a troublemaker in school, so technically, Daniel became his only friend. Daniel loved using his brains and was found to be a multitalented student. He always managed his time well. Despite having bullies, Daniel never fought others, and controlled his rage whenever possible. He took karate lessons with a martial artist named Mr Wong who also taught him Kung-fu. Daniel spent hours creating his own kung-fu technique, the 'tiger fist' which was a combination of the dragon fist and the tiger technique.

One day, a new student arrived at Daniel's art class. Daniel couldn't help looking at her continuously. She had wavy blonde hair, beautiful green eyes and a cheerful face.

"Who's the new girl?" asked Daniel as both he and Alfred sat together for lunch.

"Her name is Angel" Alfred replied. "Angel Keller. She comes from New York. Her hobbies are"

"You've been reading her file, haven't you?" asked Daniel, who wasn't amused by Alfred's surprising information.

"Well, a little." Alfred said, nervously. "Don't tell anyone though. By the way, why did you ask?"

"I was just curious." Daniel answered with his eyes fixed on Angel.

"Don't lie to me, Dan." Said Alfred. "Your eyes are fixed on her. You like her!"

"Nice try, trickster." Said Daniel, remaining as calm as ever.

"Oh, and her boyfriend is Arnold Grey." Alfred added.

"The class bully?!" shouted Daniel who was stained with shock. Arnold was an upperclassman and is the self proclaimed strongest and coolest teen in school. He had several encounters with Daniel, making them fierce rivals.

"Yeah, I know! I spat out some of my drink when I first knew." Alfred said. "Wow, you are so concerned about her all of a sudden."

"Don't push your luck, Al" said Daniel, all of a sudden hard-heartedly.

"I was just joking." Said Alfred, "although, it's true."

"Let's just drop this now." Daniel said after a moment.

He took his tray and went towards the trash can. On his left, Angel was sitting with Arnold and his friend, Derek who was whispering something to Arnold when he spotted Daniel walking by. He placed his foot in the way for Daniel to trip. Daniel knew this but he decided to fall into their trap. He balanced himself when he tripped, making Arnold, Derek, and Angel astonished.

"Hey! I'm going to tell Washington a piece of my mind." Arnold whispered to Derek."In the meantime, you show Angel around."

Chapter 5

A New Friend and a New Enemy

Daniel was getting ready for arts class, but was halted by Arnold.

"Listen, Washington!" shouted Arnold, grabbing Daniel on the jacket. "If you ever spoil my reputation that costs me Angel, I will make your nose bleed."

"Look, if you want to fight you're asking the wrong person." said Daniel. "Now, get your hands off me."

He held Arnold's hand firmly, making him wince in pain. Arnold quickly released Daniel's jacket.

"You will suffer for this later" Arnold threatened.

So Angel doesn't know much about Arnold, Daniel thought as he grinned wryly.

After school, Angel walked with Arnold. She then spotted Daniel doing some odd kung- Fu moves. Angel decided to stay behind a little longer.

Daniel gave a palm blow at a nearby tree, knocking down the eight apples that hung on it. He then took a bite of an apple while sitting down under the tree.

"Impressive!" exclaimed Angel. Daniel jumped back a bit.

"Sorry to startle you. That was amazing what you did just now."

"Uh, thanks. Want one?" asked Daniel, offering her an apple.

"No, thank you." Angel said. "What do you call that move?"

"It's a combination of the tiger technique and dragon fist." Daniel said. "I call it the tiger fist. Want to learn?"

"How about tomorrow?" suggested Angel.

"No problem, I'm Daniel by the way." He reached out shyly with his right hand.

"Angel Keller. See you tomorrow." Angel said, shaking his hand, and quickly walked away. Daniel continued to eat his apples as he waited for his limousine to come.

Later that day, Daniel was down at the basement, delivering punches to a punching bag. He eventually burst the bag whilst dealing mentally with some financial issues. Mr. Wong then showed up and soon both he and Daniel were training intensely in Kung- Fu.

"Now, show me what you have learnt." ordered Mr Wong as he stood in his fighting stance.

"Alright." Replied Daniel as he took up his fighting stance. They both fought for a long period of time. Daniel used the tiger fist technique he had practiced at a very fast pace that overwhelmed Mr Wong, sending him flying over the side of the ring.

"Are you okay, sir?" asked Daniel. Wong got up.

"Impressive! You have passed, my student." He said proudly. "Your next lesson will be the twisting tiger technique."

"Well, this has to be cool." said Daniel.

He also learned how to control and release his inner strength and energy. Mr. Wong informed him that his rage was the only thing that would release his inner strength. Soon, Mr. Wong left.

Later that day, Daniel told John about his day.

"I don't know how long I can control my rage" he complained. "If this continues, I am going to lose it one day, and there will be no one on this earth who could stop me!"

"What is the solution, then?" asked John.

"You have to understand, father" Daniel replied "I am a Tigerton. There was a reason why I was given this and I want to find that reason."

"We will find out more about this Tigerton beast, but you have no idea what.." John started.

"You are afraid that I might get killed." Daniel interrupted.

"Exactly," John exclaimed.

"Father, you don't know what I am capable of doing! No blade, or bullet can pierce my skin!" Daniel shouted.

"This is madness, Daniel!" John snapped.

"Look at the rate of stealing in this country." Daniel said as his canines grew slightly due to his rage. "The police can't always be reliable. Someone must punish these thugs."

"Control yourself, Daniel!" John snapped. "You can also kill someone with that rage."

"I don't have any intentions of killing anybody." Daniel said as his canines decreased in size. "I can now control my anger."

"I will decide later but now let's drop the case" John concluded.

Daniel returned to the basement to continue his training as a Tigerton. After he transformed to one he engaged in Kung Fu, and Karate, and concentrated on creating his own techniques.

The next day, John woke up to find Daniel lifting weights while drinking coffee.

"How long have you been exercising?" John asked, taking a sip of his cappuccino.

"The whole night," Daniel answered. "Check this out."

He jumped ten feet off the ground in a hop. John chocked at this, and spat out some of his cappuccino. Daniel, who had been mastering his speed, moved at supersonic speed using a bucket to accurately catch the regurgitated cappuccino.

"Y-you moved at the speed of sound!" John exclaimed.

"I think so" Daniel replied as he looked at his watch.

"Yikes! School starts in three minutes."

"Forget it!" John shouted suddenly.

"I can't, I'm sure I can make it" Daniel grinned.

"Unless you're going to run to school at supersonic speed, you are too late already" John observed as Daniel finished his coffee.

"See you later!" Daniel shouted as he rushed past John.

He came to a screeching halt on the way when he saw Alfred being beaten up by Derek and his small band of bullies.

"Where's Washington?" asked Derek, hurling a blow to Alfred's stomach.

"I-I don't know." Alfred replied weakly. His face was swollen by the punches given to him earlier.

"You're lying!" Derek shouted as he caught hold of Alfred. "Tell me!"

Daniel started to clench his fists and grit his teeth. He then had an idea. If he ran at supersonic speed and fought the bullies, they will not know what had hit them. He started making funny noises that made Alfred and the bullies jump out of their skins.

"Who's there?" Derek asked. A rush of wind was the reply. He turned around to see all of his friends lying on the ground, groaning in agony.

"What trickery is this?" Derek asked, shaking poor Alfred.

"I am just as surprised as you are." Alfred answered, innocently. Then, another rush of wind came, and Derek suddenly disappeared in a blink.

Alfred was now so scared that he fainted slowly. When he woke up, he was lying in the sick bay.

Later that day, Daniel went to look for Angel to start teaching her Kung Fu. In a twist of luck, he ran into Arnold. Actually, it was Arnold who ran into him.

"Hey, watch... It's you!" Arnold spluttered. Daniel didn't have time for more trash talking.

"Um, sorry. Have you seen Angel?" Daniel asked politely.

"What do you want with her?" Arnold asked, suspiciously. Before Daniel could answer, Angel came around the corner.

"You look...prepared." Daniel managed to say.

"Prepared for what?" Arnold asked. Things are getting very suspicious nowadays.

"He's going to teach me kung fu." Angel said, quickly. Daniel watched Arnold, hoping he would blow his stack and Angel will finally know about his true colours.

"Yes. I'll be waiting outside the school gates" Arnold said, almost through gritted teeth. As Daniel and Angel left, Daniel saw Arnold kicking his locker. What's the big deal with upperclassmen nowadays?

Daniel started teaching Angel Kung Fu. Angel was a very fast learner, which made it easy for Daniel to teach.

"Wow, you're really fast at learning."

"Thanks. You are an excellent teacher" Angel replied.

"How about trying tomorrow?" Daniel asked. "Or are you busy?"

"I'll try. Arnold doesn't like the idea, though" Angel replied as she looked at Arnold, talking to Derek.

"See you tomorrow, then!" Daniel called as Angel left. He then ran home, reaching hyper sonic speed in less than three seconds. John was really getting tired of Daniel disappearing and reappearing like a ghost.

"Can't you, at least, act like a normal person?" John asked as Daniel started eating a large piece of chicken.

"I'm trying but I just can't." Daniel replied, taking another large bite of the chicken. "I don't know how much I can take."

"Anyway, I read about your Tigerton species."

"Can you please tell me?"

"Well, they are an extinct race of a creature that is close to being a member of the Panther a genus cat family" John explained. "The two last Tigerton in existence were Amaeron and Dabiasto."

Daniel then had a flashback of what the monks of the old temple in China had told him.

"It must have been Amaeron. He must have been the Tigerton who killed my parents, and turned me into this monster."

"Did those monks tell you about Dabiasto?" John asked, showing some of the pictures he'd developed on the internet to Daniel. "The taller one is Amaeron and the fierce one is Dabiasto."

"I was told that he was my opposite." Daniel replied. "He appears in my nightmares. He was Amaeron's brother."

"It is believed that he is still alive." John said. This made Daniel jump in surprise.

Chapter 6

An Unexpected Clash

Two months later, there was a big school party taking place. Daniel volunteered to help set the party up, and make it look like an all-day party.

Alfred had the special honour to be the D.J. There were lots of pupils and friends. Daniel was hoping to have a chat with Angel, but Arnold seemed to have her attention.

Suddenly, time stopped for Daniel as he sensed danger coming. With his sharp eyes, he spotted a U.F.O (Unidentified Flying Object) hundreds of feet in the air, and several robots that looked like Tigertons were jumping out of it.

"What's going on?" Alfred asked, as the machine he used was going haywire.

The pupils looked on with astonishment as the robots marched towards them.

"They must be the surprising entertainers!" A pupil shouted. The pupils cheered for the robots except for Daniel, who knew that they were all in danger.

He quickly ran to a very quiet corner and tried to be confident to transform. Meanwhile, Arnold went forward to the Tigerton robots.

"What do you think you're doing here, metal freak?" He teased, making the others laugh.

"Programming initiated." The robot droned, as he converted its robotic hand into a gun. "Move or be exterminated."

"You've got to be kidding me!" Derek said knocking the metal plate of the robot. The robot retaliated by lifting Derek, throwing him at Arnold. Angel went across to help them.

"State your business here." Alfred demanded.

"Are you the supporting act?"

"Data shows none of your business, human." The robot replied. "Move aside or consider yourself annihilated!"

"Tigerton Drone 111, hold your fire!" A deep, gruff voice from the spacecraft bellowed. A giant Tigerton jumped from the spacecraft and landed, shaking the earth.

"What is THAT thing?" shrieked Alfred, looking at the fearful face of the Tigerton. Daniel looked in shock. It was Dabiasto. Now, he must use what Amaeron had given to him. He transformed slowly into a Tigerton.

"Tell us what you want" Alfred said impatiently. "What kind of a day is this?"

"He's here" Dabiasto muttered with a smirk. A thunder-like roar was heard.

"What's that?" Angel asked who was now stiff with fright. The answer came as Tiger Fist was seen on a large building, snarling.

"It's Tiger Fist!" A student exclaimed. Most of the students cheered for Tiger Fist. Dabiasto then wore his power radar that looked like red sun glasses, and faced Tiger Fist.

"Humph." He disappeared and reappeared on the building next to Tiger Fist.

"Well, Amaeron, you've gotten far weaker than I remembered."

"You must be mistaking me for him" Tiger Fist replied. He then let out a roar that broke the windows of every building in range. "I am Tiger Fist!"

"So Amaeron gave you his 'powers" Dabiasto smirked. "Tigerton Drones, attack!"

The drones started shooting at Tiger Fist's direction. He jumped down from the building and at the speed of sound, he fought the drones. To the students' eyes, Tiger Fist was a brown blur of wind destroying every drone that was in his way. Dabiasto knew that Tiger Fist couldn't be affected by normal bullets.

Tiger Fist turned to glare at Dabiasto and lunged at him. Before he could attack, Dabiasto gave him a slap, which felt like a bowling ball to Tiger Fist. The slap sent him to a skyscraper, which then collapsed on him. The students gave a petrified gasp, believing he was dead.

The police had been called but every constable was killed by the collapsing skyscraper. To everyone's shock, except for Dabiasto, Daniel jumped out of the wreckage. Dabiasto taunted him for a few moments. Tiger Fist fell for it and Dabiasto grabbed him by the tail.

"You rely too much on strength and speed alone" Dabiasto said. He then swung Tiger Fist in a spinning fashion and threw him to the ground, creating a massive hole.

"He can't even touch him." Angel whispered, as she helped Arnold to his feet.

Tiger Fist jumped out of nowhere. He paused for a moment.

'I must outwit him, somehow.'
An idea came to him. He started to rub his hands together as fast as he could. Within a minute, his hands were on fire. This made the students and Dabiasto speechless.

"Of course!" exclaimed Alfred. "He withstood enormous friction between his paws or hands. That's how he made fire."

Dabiasto overheard Alfred, and then did the same thing, but Tiger Fist showed no sign of surprise. He clapped his 'paws' together, creating a wave of fire. Dabiasto tried to imitate him, but couldn't make any waves. However, Dabiasto evaded the fire. Tiger Fist then lunged at Dabiasto, giving him a solid punch to the chest and an uppercut to the chin.

Dabiasto crashed into a car. He lost his temper and ran towards Tiger Fist. Tiger Fist was prepared, and dodged

Dabiasto's offenses. He has now learnt to rely on his Tigerton senses. He grabbed Dabiasto by the tail, swung him around and threw him to the spacecraft.

"You're not so powerful now, eh Dabiasto?" Tiger Fist growled. The student cheered.

Dabiasto looked down from the spacecraft. "Humph! This is nothing but a test. These drones were my first models. I have several others that are eight times more powerful."

Tiger Fist couldn't believe his ears. This fight was just a stupid set-up which had cost lives of Los Angeles police officers officers, and the destruction of several buildings. He clenched his paws.

"We will meet again, Amaeron!" Dabiasto roared as the spacecraft disappeared into the clouds.

The students cheered for Tiger Fist. When Angel looked at him, Tiger Fist bent his face downwards, pretending to have something in his eyes. Once he secretly transformed back to normal, Daniel left the party. He went back to his mansion. He met John, his arms crossed and the news was on, showing the recent fight. Blast!

"Hello, Dad." Daniel said, weakly.

"Hello, Son." John replied with a whole different look on his face. "Can you please explain why CNN TV is showing footage of a fight between two extraterrestrial mutated tigers?"

"I had every good reason to fight!" Daniel snapped.

"You're kidding me, right?!" John shouted, who was now flared up. "You disobeyed me, took on a robotic army and destroyed seven buildings in the process. ARE YOU EVEN LISTENING?!"

Daniel roared in response, got so angry that he transformed into a Tiger Fist. "Dabiasto planned this destruction! I was the only one who stood up to him! After fighting, he revealed that this was a test! Who are you now going to put the blame on?"

"So he was testing you?" John asked, intimidated by Tiger Fist for a bit. "That means…"

"He knows all about me" Tiger Fist interjected. "I need to train more, and fast!"

"Wait a minute!" John called. "First of all, I need to study you a bit and second of all, you are asking to get killed!"

"Why do you underestimate me?" Tiger Fist asked. "What must I do to prove that I am invulnerable?"

He picked up a metal bar and gave it to John.

"What should I do with this?" John asked.

"Hit me as hard as you can."

"No, I won't." John said reluctantly. Tiger Fist sighed and started hitting himself with the bar.

The bar eventually broke into tiny pieces.

John fainted, for the first time in his life. He woke up to see Tiger Fist transform back to Daniel.

"What have I done?" John asked. "All this time, you were the key to make the world a better place."

"Well, that's what I've been trying to tell you." Daniel said impatiently. "I need to train for my next clash with Dabiasto, but I don't have the materials I need."

"Hang on. I used to be a scientist in Hampshire, England a long time ago. I have a PhD in Engineering and Chemistry."

"And it's only now you're telling me?" Daniel asked, thinking that John had suddenly lost his mind.

"I think I have the tools you need deep in the basement." John said, heading to the basement. Daniel sighed and arrived at the basement before John. John finally entered the basement.

He picked up a hammer, intending to break the wall behind the gym. Daniel stopped him.

"Allow the big guy to do it." He said, transforming into Tiger Fist. He pierced the wall with his index finger, breaking the entire wall instantly.

"I should get used to that." John replied as he started to rummage over the old tools. "What we need now are things you can, and cannot lift."

"My strength has no limits" Tiger Fist reminded him. "I can get stronger at will."

"I have an idea!" John exclaimed. "I have a friend who has over several tons of titanium. He has never found any use for it. Let me see if I can get in contact with him."

It took John two hours to convince his friend to give him the titanium. Daniel was allowed to go back to the party, but he found that most of the students had left.

"Why did the party finish so early?" Daniel asked Alfred, who was about to head for home.

"The amplifiers wouldn't work, so the party had to end" Alfred answered.

"Did Angel leave?" Daniel asked after a quick look around.

"Yep, she went to the hospital with Arnold." Alfred answered. "By the way, where were you when this 'Tiger Fist' guy showed up?"

"I was getting a drink." Daniel lied. He was really disappointed that he didn't get enough time to at least talk to her.

"If it hurts you that much, I'll give you her number" Alfred offered.

"How to goodness did you get that?" Daniel asked, now too surprised to be disappointed.

"Found it on the note Arnold dropped."

"Thanks, man!" Daniel exclaimed, as Alfred gave him the note.

"Well, I have to be going. Later!"

Chapter 7

Intense Training for a Tigerton

The next day, John returned with his friend's unwanted titanium. Daniel was chatting with Angel on the phone, and looked with disgust at the giant block of titanium.

"How are we ever going to use this, Dad?" He asked.

"I think I can convert it into gymnastic gears" John said. "Try and lift it."

Daniel transformed into Tiger Fist, tearing through his fifth T-shirt of the day. He grabbed the titanium and succeeded in lifting it. He grunted at the weight of the metal.

"I've never lifted something so heavy before." He grumbled.

"Well, that's what you'll be lifting after I convert it." John answered slyly.

"How long will that take?" Tiger Fist asked, as he placed the heavy titanium carefully on the ground.

"In about two days." John replied.

"I will transform back to normal."

"Don't transform yet!" John yelled. "You will train as Tiger Fist."

Tiger Fist began his intensive training. He trained for two days straight. He grew stronger and far more athletic for his size. He also developed his Tigerton senses; he can smell something from more than a mile away.

John made a giant bench press and a giant metal ball with the titanium. He began to use them effectively.

In the corner of the room, a spy robotic spider crawled up the wall transmitting images of Tiger Fist training to Dabiasto's monitor. He looked at the screen, almost in anger.

"So he thinks he can surpass me." Dabiasto sneered. "I will undertake some training of my own."

"Your training courses are ready" A robotic Tigerton called T-139 confirmed.

Dabiasto started training with his electronic suit, and started a more complex workout. The T-robots had their own training especially target practice.

Meanwhile, John was given permission to use thirty carriages at the railway station. Daniel would pull the coaches while running on the railway track. He did so while running at a hundred miles per hour. For his next work, he would lift each carriage forty times.

Later that day, Daniel visited the hospital where he found Angel sitting beside an unconscious Arnold.

"How bad is he?" Daniel asked.

"He's been unconscious for two days" Angel said, close to tears. Daniel patted her on the shoulder. He then spotted a robotic spider under Arnold's hand. He carefully opened the hand and took it.

"What's this?" Daniel asked.

"It's a spy toy used to, you know, spy." Angel replied. "I wonder why he has it."

Daniel gave a sniff and his green eyes glowed. He looked closely at the spy toy. He saw the insignia of toy as a red painted eye. Then, a flashback of Dabiasto came to him. Daniel's eyes grew wide.

"How long has he… never mind." He looked at Arnold's skin. It was too pale for someone to be alive. He touched his skin.

"That's funny." Daniel said.

"What?" Angel asked.

"What kind of a body feels like metal?" Daniel asked knocking Arnold's covered body. He removed the cover to find out that this Arnold was a robot and that the real Arnold works for Dabiasto. Angel gave a petrified gasp. Daniel snarled a bit.

He glared at Angel. "What's going on? This doesn't make any sense."

Angel looked solemnly back. "I don't know. The doctor said nothing about this."

"Perhaps he escaped from the hospital without being seen, right?" Daniel suggested.

"Why would he think of doing that?" Angel asked.

"That's just a suggestion" Daniel grinned, although this was not the time for grinning. He needed to know what connection Arnold had with Dabiasto.

"Try contacting him, and check his house." Daniel added

"Okay. Bye!" Angel called as Daniel left the hospital, and headed back home.

"Dad, Arnold's working for Dabiasto." Daniel blurted. "He's been spying on us and giving information to Dabiasto."

"Where is he now?"

"He's probably with Dabiasto." As he went to the basement for more workouts, he was halted by a voice.

"You used your powers so foolishly that you don't know who gave it to you."

"Who are you?" Daniel asked. Everything he saw was a jungle and in front of him was a large, old-looking Tigerton, glaring at him.

"Y-you look like me." Daniel added.

"No. You look like me." The Tigerton said. Daniel couldn't believe his eyes.

"You're Amaeron." Daniel said. "You're the one who killed my parents for no reason and put this curse on me."

"I spent five millennia looking for the perfect living thing to give my powers, and here you are saying it's a curse?"

"Was it necessary to kill my parents?" Daniel asked, transforming into Tiger Fist when he thought of his parents.

"That's the power" Amaeron said, proudly. "You will

understand one day that a Tigerton does not lament for its dead."

"Well, I'm not going to lament when I kill you!" Tiger Fist pounced at Amaeron who simply moved out of the way.

"Dabiasto would have killed me because I am too old to fight. I had to transfer my powers to a young and brave living thing."

Tiger Fist cooled down. "How do I beat Dabiasto? He's stronger, faster and smarter than I will ever be."

"No. That's not true. Use your instincts." And with that, Amaeron disappeared and the green surrounding was back to normal. Daniel's phone rang. It was Arnold.

"Washington, you have to get over here!" Arnold panicked. "Angel's been kidnapped!"

"Alright, I'm coming!" Daniel answered and without a second thought, he ran to Angel's house. He met Arnold, comforting Angel's mother, Alice Keller.

"That was fast" Arnold said. "Mrs Keller, allow me to introduce my friend, Lawrence Washington."

"It's Daniel" Daniel said, politely. "Can I ask what happened?"

"Dabiasto took her" Arnold answered.

"So, you've been his accomplice all along" Daniel said.

"Look, he set me up when I agreed to spy on you" Arnold admitted, innocently.

"Well, you can tell me where Dabiasto is, then" Daniel said, feeling very clever.

"Dabiasto will kill me if I do" Arnold squealed.

"It is for the good of Angel" Daniel said who started to get impatient as Arnold hesitated.

"I've never seen such a beast in my life!" Alice shrieked. "He ransacked the place, and took my daughter!"

"Don't worry; I will bring her safely back to you." Daniel reassured her.

"How are you going to do that?"

"I will find a way."

"You're a kind boy."

Arnold told him about Dabiasto's laboratory in Greenland. Daniel left the house, feeling really angry at the thought of Dabiasto kidnapping Angel.

"Daniel, what is it?" John asked as Daniel barged into the room.

"Angel's been kidnapped by Dabiasto" Daniel replied, fuming.

"This is bad!" John exclaimed. "Where is he right now?"

"He has a laboratory in Greenland. I have to go now!"

"Don't you think you're falling into a trap? After all, Dabiasto is not a fool."

"I know. There is no escaping that trap, but I will find a way."

"Alright, good luck and be careful" John said, patting Daniel on the back.

Chapter 8

The Battle of the Tigertons

Daniel took off his clothes, wearing only elastic trunks. He transformed into Tiger Fist, and started on his way to Greenland. With his supersonic speed and his Tigerton senses, he soon found himself in front of the laboratory. Greenland is a very cold island, covered entirely with snow but Tiger Fist adapted to the cold and hid in a mound of snow. The laboratory was guarded by hundreds of T-robots and Tiger Fist assumed that the robots had enhanced invulnerability and weaponry.

Tiger Fist ambushed the robots with a leap of surprise. He dodged the bullets fired by the robots and dismantled them. Dabiasto watched this frantic operation intensely on his monitor. He didn't expect his assailant to be this strong

Tiger Fist dug his way underground into the laboratory. He then faced six of the much improved T-robots. It wasn't easy for him, but he soon destroyed the robots, and went on. He came upon a deadly maze of traps.

'*Maybe I can run fast enough to avoid triggering the traps*' Tiger Fist thought to himself. He did so, and managed to succeed in not triggering the traps.

"Impressive!" Dabiasto said. He was seeing Tiger Fist's action with the help of security cameras. "Let's see if he can attack this."

Tiger Fist suddenly stopped to a halt. He was picking up a scent of coconut on a metal. Well, whatever it was, it didn't show a good sign.

Suddenly, a giant Tigerton robot emerged from the shadows.

"You, fool!" Dabiasto's voice sounded over the speakers. "Did you really think I would just allow you to barge into my lab and leave without any reason?"

"Don't play coy with me" Tiger Fist growled. "You're holding an innocent girl hostage so that you can lure me into a trap."

"Well, let's see if you can take one of my greatest robots, T-190 Mark 2."

"I'll let you know when I do some serious thrashing to your oversized toy" Tiger Fist grinned.

The T-190 gave a loud monotone growl that created sound waves.

"*That robot's roar is too much for my comfort, but I have to be careful about those sound waves.*" Tiger Fist dodged the attack but found it difficult to penetrate the T-robot's metal body.

"What kind of metal is this robot made from?" Tiger Fist asked after recovering from a powerful swipe of the 18 foot robot.

"Ninety eight per cent of the robot is made of a rare and enchanted metal called invincium" Dabiasto answered unexpectedly.

"Well, in that case, I have to think out of the box for this one." Tiger Fist grinned after realizing that the chest plate of the robot was made of glass. He gave a giant leap in the air and landed on the T-190's chest plate. He broke the glass with a punch. The T-190 immediately deactivated and fell to the ground.

Tiger Fist continued to explore the never-ending lab. He finally picked up Angel's scent and went through a highly protected path. He found Angel, with her arms in chains and kept in a visible electromagnetic force field. However, there was no sign of Dabiasto or any robots. But, before Tiger Fist could move any further, Dabiasto appeared with thirteen T-robots.

"It's about time you came here, Amaeron" Dabiasto said.

"Amaeron is not my name" Tiger Fist growled. "I am Tiger Fist, Amaeron's half-son."

"Well, you'd better be a good entertainer" Dabiasto said, as six doors opened and fifty T-robots came out of each door. These T-robots looked different from the ones he had faced.

"These are my fourth greatest T-robots." Dabiasto explained. "I call them the T-191 Mark 4. They are made of invincium and are invulnerable to any physical attack. They can survive for days in a volcano."

"I hope they come with an 'off' switch" Tiger Fist laughed.

"T-robots, attack!" Dabiasto commanded.

Tiger Fist still couldn't penetrate the invincium metal. The robots were equipped with plasma cannons and began blasting at Tiger Fist.

"I want to get stronger than this" Tiger Fist growled to himself. He soon realized that his biceps, quadriceps and other various muscles in his body had increased in size. Dabiasto wore his energy reader and looked at Tiger Fist.

"His strength is increasing more than four hundred times before."

Tiger Fist roared in anger. He pounded the ground in a rage, splitting the lab in two. In a blink of an eye, Tiger Fist tore each T-robot apart, causing them to deactivate.

"Don't you have anymore?!" Tiger Fist snarled.

"Are you serious?" Dabiasto asked. Two doors opened and seven clones of Tiger Fist appeared.

Tiger Fist looked in disbelief. "I don't believe this."

"They have unlimited strength and regeneration. So you see it's impossible to defeat my minions." Dabiasto boasted.

Tiger Fist began pummelling the clones without any remorse. Dabiasto felt very uneasy from where he was sitting. Tiger Fist was getting stronger every second.

Tiger Fist finally defeated the clones when he realized that his roar can produce sound waves , which affect the clones' sensors, causing them to deactivate. It was Dabiasto's turn to fuel with rage.

"Is that it? Is there anymore?" Tiger Fist roared.

"So you still ask for more?" Dabiasto taunted. "You will soon kneel at my feet, begging for your life. But first, there is someone I want you to fight."

Out of a door came a familiar human in a suit of titanium armour. Tiger Fist glared at the person. Angel eyes went wide with surprise. Even with her mouth taped, her gasp could be heard.

"So you made me come here so that you can fight me, Arnold?" Tiger Fist sneered.

"Don't take me for a fool, Washington" Arnold said, "I know of your powers better than you can imagine."

"So I hope you wouldn't be stupid enough to face me" Tiger Fist scoffed. Suddenly, Arnold withdrew two plasma whips, and cracked them like horsewhips.

"Do you know that a Tigerton's only weakness is the powerful slashes of a plasma whip?" Arnold chuckled as he cracked the whips while moving towards Tiger Fist.

"Let's bash and thrash." Tiger Fist rushed towards Arnold in a heartbeat and delivered a heavy swipe of his big paw at Arnold that sent him flying to the air. From the look of things, he seemed to have killed him. Tiger Fist hadn't felt guilty of his action until he looked at Angel's tear filled eyes. To his surprise, Arnold got up and lashed out with his plasma whips.

Tiger Fist easily dodged the whips since he can react to danger quicker than a normal Tigerton.

"Stand still for a minute" Arnold demanded after wearing himself out.

"Ha! How's this?" Tiger Fist wanted to test the power of the plasma whip.

"Perfect" Arnold smirked and lashed out with both whips at Tiger Fist. Tiger Fist accurately caught the whip and began to grunt in agony. He had never felt pain in his life. He slowly lost his strength.

"Fool! No Tigerton, not even me, can resist the pain of the plasma whip!" Dabiasto shouted. He then cast a look at Angel's worried eyes as she stared at Tiger Fist. "And we'll make sure Angel joins you when you meet with your Maker."

As Tiger Fist looked in Angel's eyes, his anger returned to him, reviving the strength that he'd lost. He got to his feet and yanked the whips out of Arnold's hands. He then broke the whips in half.

This sent Arnold, Angel and Dabiasto into a great shock. As he cooled down, Tiger Fist was surprised at himself. He soon realized that he had no physical weakness.

"But how can you-?" Arnold asked, trembling all over.

"I am Tiger Fist, the greatest Tigerton to ever exist." Tiger Fist answered.

Dabiasto, now furious, jumped from the platform he was standing on and landed near Arnold. Arnold begged for forgiveness for he had failed him. Without any remorse, Dabiasto killed Arnold with a swipe of a paw.

He then faced Tiger Fist. Due to the great increase in strength because of his recent fights, Tiger Fist was physically bigger and bulkier than Dabiasto.

"What's the matter?" Tiger Fist mocked. "Lost your tongue?"

"It is your tongue that needs to be cut! What you see is only my normal form."

"Let's see how strong you are." They both started to fight at a speed faster than the human eye could see. That meant Angel could not see them fighting, but could only hear the growls and thrashing.

Learning to trust his instincts, Tiger Fist could sense anytime Dabiasto wants to attack. With a powerful swipe, Tiger Fist sent Dabiasto crashing into walls.

Realizing his inadequate strength, Dabiasto decided to transform into an even more brutal version. At this rate, Dabiasto was now two inches taller than Tiger Fist, and thus more bulky.

The two Tigertons then clashed again. It seemed that one could not surpass the other. Tiger Fist relied on his speed and kept punching Dabiasto. He later gave him a kick to the gut that temporarily disabled him.

Dabiasto then increased in strength, invulnerability and speed. As he was transforming, Tiger Fist rubbed his paws together so fast his paws emitted sparks, and then fire. He then clapped his hands together, creating a powerful tongue of fire that caused an explosion when it touched Dabiasto.

As the dust cleared, Dabiasto wasn't harmed in any way. Tiger Fist had expected that but couldn't resist his fire action.

"I'm tired of your games, you son of Amaeron!" Dabiasto snarled.

"Alright, let's see how you deal with this!" Tiger Fist yelled.

Tiger Fist started to spin so fast that he, along with the cool air in the laboratory, turned into a tornado. The tornado moved slowly, causing the lab to fall apart. Dabiasto looked in horror at the state of his lab. He ran quickly towards the tornado, but was hit by Tiger Fist's rotating arms. Dabiasto then rammed Tiger Fist, and finally stopped the tornado.

"Look, what you've done to my lab!" Dabiasto bellowed. The lab was definitely in bad shape. All the apparatus, mechanical and electronic machines were destroyed. Angel managed to break free since the force field was dismantled.

Tiger Fist struggled to his feet. He had been fighting without rest for fourteen hours and was now in need of food. That could definitely not be said for Dabiasto.

In a rage, he started to thrash the weakened Tiger Fist and kicked him to a pillar. Dabiasto then wore an energy regenerating machine and his eyes shone.

"Enjoy this plasma beam!" He shouted and he released a large ray of plasma at Tiger Fist. Tiger Fist regenerated and crawled towards a pillar. Dabiasto grabbed his neck. "You don't deserve this power. So looks like you die with it!"

"NO!" Angel screamed. She was holding a plasma gun. "Stay away from him!"

Dabiasto laughed. "And if I don't?"

Without a second warning, Angel shot Dabiasto with the plasma gun. He roared in pain.

Taking advantage of this useful distraction, Tiger Fist recovered his energy, and punched Dabiasto. He then took in a deep breath to produce a supersonic roar.

"RAAAARGH!"

The earth splitting roar produced sound waves strong enough to destroy the laboratory, and send Dabiasto flying to the far corner of Greenland, where he froze in an icy pool.

Tiger Fist then rescued Angel from of the collapsing lab. Once outside, he put Angel down and collapsed in the snow to catch a breath. Angel looked at him closely.

"Daniel, is that you?" She asked. Tiger Fist knew that she had been through a lot lately, so he couldn't keep anymore secrets from her.
"Yes. Under this creature is Daniel" he confessed.
"Do you think that monster will be back?"
"Sadly, yes. I believe this isn't the last I will see of him."
"Let's get out of here."
"You're right."

Tiger Fist picked Angel up, and took her home to America. As Daniel, he delivered Angel to her mother and watched both of them enjoy their happy reunion.

Afterwards, Daniel returned to the mansion and sat down on a chair.

"What a day! I think I'm going to take a long nap."

And that's what he did. Daniel knew that a hero's job wasn't easy, but taking a nap was the least he could do after what had happened throughout that memorable day.

Chapter 9

How It Ends

Three months later, Tiger Fist became a worldwide phenomenon. As Daniel read the reviews and critics' comment, Angel was at his side. Not long after the defeat of Dabiasto, John went on vacation with Daniel, Alfred and Angel to Nepal. They toured a lot.

"So, you finally got the girl." Alfred whispered to Daniel.

As Daniel looked up at Mount Everest, a grin came across his face.

"Ten dollars if I climb mount Everest" he joked with Alfred.

"Have you lost your mind? You're on!" Alfred exclaimed. Without a second thought, Daniel started hopping to the top.

"What's he doing?" John asked.

"He's having fun" Angel answered.

As he leapt several feet in the air landing on the snowy slope, half way up Mount Everest, Daniel thought about his new role as a real super hero.

THE END

GLOSSARY

Tigerton - An extinct species of hybrids of a tiger and a human.

Anubulaen - An extinct species of hybrids of a wolf and man.

T-robots - Robots created by Dabiasto and are modelled after him.

The Legend of Chrumesteeler

Author's Note

After finding out that people were interested in reading my first story, I decided to write another. What if my hero fought an enemy who had an empire and proved to be nearly invincible? Now that's a story for young people to read. I hope this story serves as a lesson that on any road to victory, the potholes are always deep. When one encounters problems on the road to success, no matter how impossible they seem, it pays to continue to believe in oneself, and maintain full determination.

Summary

The Tigerton is back and his life is crazier than ever. However, the problems are even worse as a legendary king threatened many lives and Alfred had been acting strange. Will Tiger Fist put his mind over matter or has his fate been sealed? In these pages I hope to provide all the answers.

Chapter 1

Struggle between Two

Across the State of California, peace and love reigned in the hearts of its citizens; well, at least most of the time. The people thanked someone living amongst them who also enjoyed every bit of the peaceful atmosphere he had brought to the State. And that someone was none other than the mighty Tiger Fist. Every day, he would sniff out any trouble that lurked around the streets of the State cities. To everyone that knew him, there was nothing he could not do, and no problem he could not solve.

Every thug in Los Angeles and the other cities feared him. No matter how hard they tried, or what weapons they used, they could not make Tiger Fist break a sweat. Being a hero also came with criticism. So many critics thought Tiger Fist's efforts were meaningless and unnecessary, and that the police were more suitable for the job. Despite this, Tiger Fist pointed out that peace had nothing to do with being the better person and he continued with his 'work'. Once he was satisfied that Los Angeles was safe for a while, he would go to San Francisco and the other cities to help stop natural disasters, robberies, and other problems.

However, people did not know that the vigilante Tiger Fist had an alternative personality. Every day, Tiger Fist would go to the mansion of John Washington where he transformed himself into a boy named Daniel Washington. After finally having permission from John to save the world, Daniel balanced his two lives carefully and enjoyed the day without regret.

"Father, how's your latest invention?" Daniel asked one day as he entered John's new laboratory.

"Well, there it is." John answered as he took out two large boots. "This is what I call the 'Tiger Jet Boosters'."

"Let me guess." Daniel said. "They will enable me to fly."

"Good guess." John said. "They could also convert into any other types of shoes in the world."

"Amazing, but why are they striped like a tiger?"

"You didn't think that these were for your human form, did you?" John asked. Daniel quickly understood what John was saying. He then spotted a giant vest made of wires.

"Let me guess." Daniel said, studying the wired vest. "This is also for Tiger Fist."

"You speak as if he was a different person." John corrected. "This vest is made of electric wires. You can use it to train now."

"Let's see if it fits." Daniel piped with excitement. By shouting 'Tiger Fist', he quickly transformed himself into a Tigerton without any sign of aggression. This surprised John.

"You can you transform by just saying the name?" he asked. "How did you ever figure that out?"

"Amaeron gave me some tips." Tiger Fist answered.

"Amaeron speaks to you even when he's dead?"

"It must be Tigerton telepathy or something." Tiger Fist answered impatiently. John noticed this reaction with a shrug. "Okay, get back to your training."

Tiger Fist wore the wired vest and started training. He practiced his karate lessons. He also practiced his own moves. He then did push-ups. As he worked through his tough training schedule, he started to think about Angel.

It had not been easy for her to recover from Arnold's murder and her kidnapping that happened two years ago. Soon afterwards, Daniel had become her boyfriend and he had tried to comfort her by going on dates, and talking to her. She continued to take karate lessons with Daniel. He could see that Angel always seemed so determined to reach perfection and to impress him.

Tiger Fist finally practiced climbing and clinging to the walls with his claws. He quickly climbed up onto the ceiling, maintaining his balance. After training, he had dinner with John while watching TV. The national news mentioned a huge decrease in crime rate in the U.S.A, and also the great developments achieved by Tiger Fist. "Oh, I forgot to turn back" he grunted. John then gave a sigh of relief as he always shuddered every time he looked at Tiger Fist. After transforming back into human, Daniel continued to devour a large drumstick.

Chapter 2

In the Land of Aeachoria

Meanwhile, an ancient country in the continent of Asia, could look back on a great past; the powerful country of Aeachoria, home of the densest metals in the world.

Aeachoria provided the origins of modern science, and advanced technology especially in the design of different types of weaponry. The country became one of the safest places on earth guarded by walls of steel. In paticular, her citizens, known as Chorians, were very experienced in the use of weaponry in war.

The common metal which the Chorians used for making suits of armour was chrome steel. In fact, Chorians wore clothes made of steel instead of fabric because their ancestors used to do just that. What made Aeachoria quite famous in the ancient world wasn't the country's wealth in metal but rather the actions of their king.

The King's name was Daien Arcrealto. But, this was not the name he used, or the name that made his historical enemies tremble. He lived by the name of 'Chrumesteeler' because he wore a suit of armour made out of an enchanted chrome steel metal; there was nothing in existence that could pierce his suit of armour.

He possessed such strength as no human could possibly imagine. His skill in weaponry was the best in the world. One day, as he sat on his large throne, he spoke with his commanders.

"Is my army ready?" he asked.

"Your soldiers are ready and await your command" Zaphuna, Commander of the northern Aeachorian soldiers, replied.

Chrumesteeler smirked. "Good, it's been two centuries since the United Kingdom betrayed us in our faces."

"Every soldier should pay with his blood." Morlan, Commander of the southern Aeachorian army, said. "My men have the best tactical weaponry in Asia... and those British have forgotten that!"

"How's my son doing with his training?" Chrumesteeler asked.

"He has so far endured his use of any modern Aeachoria weapon." Zonan, trainer of the northern Aeachorian army, replied.

Chrumesteeler rejoiced. "I hope so, because Junior is going to witness his first battle"

Just then Horuun, the court wizard and Aaron, one

of the greatest scientific geniuses in Aeachoria came to the King.

Chrumesteeler asked with a sigh. "Oh, what do you two rivals want to fight over this time?"

Horuun replied while drawing his white beard. "Aaron and I had agreed to make weapons with both magic and modern technology."

Aaron removed a mini-projector from his lab coat pocket. Several high tech weapons were projected in various parts of the throne room.

"I had designed these five years ago, but I didn't have the raw materials to make them." Aaron explained. "That is until Horuun came to my aid."

"I call this the ASC4." Aaron continued. "It has eight times the power of a normal C4 bomb. It is also easy to detonate."

"I helped to control the dangerous chemicals in this weapon." Horuun blurted out, trying to gain some attention.

"How many of the 'ASC4' did you make?" Chrumesteeler asked, impressed by the weapon's power.

"About seven hundred should be enough to ease the war." Aaron replied.

"Let's carry on with our other creations, Captain Genius." Horuun said, impatiently.

"Humph, fine." Aaron scoffed. "This battle tank is what I called the 'Aeachoria Attackers'."

"I hope you didn't just make one." Chrumesteeler said, slyly.

"On the contrary, I made fifty of them."

"How did you make so many so quickly?" Chrumesteeler asked.

"With my magic, nothing is impossible." Horuun boasted.

"I also improved on your ultra-barreled plasma gun cannons." Aaron said.

"You mean the U.B.P.G.C?" Zaphuna asked, causing the rest to laugh.

"And I made this just for you, sire." Horuun said.

With a snap of his fingers, Horuun turned Chrumesteeler's old armour into a shinier and more advanced armour.

"This suit of armour is made from the strongest metals in the world." Horuun added. "I have also enchanted it with the utmost invulnerability."

"You both will be rewarded for this, but what of my son?" Chrumesteeler asked.

"Oh, I made him a similar one like yours." Horuun replied.

"When do we leave?" Morlan asked.

"Prepare for battle now!" Chrumesteeler ordered.

Chapter 3

A Warning

While Chrumesteeler and the Chorian army prepared for battle in the other part of the world, Tiger Fist was doing some preparations of his own in Los Angeles, California, U.S.A.

"Come on, you can do it!" Angel cheered.

She and Alfred both watched Tiger Fist as he was about to make his one thousandth lift of fifty tons of chrome steel combined with ten tons of iron.

"I don't believe it!" Alfred exclaimed. It was already shocking that he now knows that Daniel was Tiger Fist but he never thought he would be so strong.

"If you didn't want me to win, why did you cheer for me?" Tiger Fist asked.

"Okay Alfred, pay up." Angel demanded.

"Here you go." Alfred said through gritted teeth as he gave Angel five dollars. Tiger Fist started punching a punching bag made out of chrome steel.

"Don't you ever get tired or feel anything?"

"I've been trying to see how invulnerable I am and I have been punching this for three months." Tiger Fist explained. "Now I feel nothing. Hit me."

Alfred gave a punch to Tiger Fist's giant six-packed stomach. Within two seconds, Alfred jumped back in pain.

Alfred groaned. "What are you made of?"

"Didn't I tell you?" Tiger Fist asked. "I am invulnerable to any human power."

Angel laughed. "Looks like the jokes on you, Alfred. What did you expect from a human-tiger mutant who spends twelve hours working out in his basement?"

With a deep sigh, Tiger Fist turned into Daniel.

"The strongest living thing in existence is my best friend." Alfred grumbled, still nursing his hand. "I wonder what it would be like if I had... wait, what are you doing, sniffing around like that?"

"Something's wrong." Daniel said, while sniffing. "My senses are tingling."

With a whoosh of wind, Daniel ran

John was watching CNN.

"Oh, you must have sensed it." John said, as he stooped back in surprise, and spotted Daniel.

"What happened?" Daniel asked.

"It seems that England is going out to war with Aeachoria." John replied.

"I don't think I've ever heard of that country before." Daniel admitted.

"Aeachoria was a country that nearly stretched throughout the world centuries ago." John continued.

"The country was ruled by a powerful man by the name Chrumesteeler."

"It sounds like more of a nickname."

"What scares people is that Chrumesteeler might still be alive and is still king."

"That's impossible."

"NO, IT'S NOT!" A loud, ear-breaking voice that Daniel was familiar with, blasted.

"What are **you** talking about, Amaeron?" Daniel asked. The sight of John and the living room faded to darkness.

Out of the darkness, a large Tigerton glared at him. "He is the ruler I would never forget."

"You know him?" Daniel asked.

"Chrumesteeler is the most powerful human that ever lived." Amaeron growled. "He is the true fear of a Tigerton."

"Ooh, I never knew a human would strike fear into the heart of the mighty Amaeron." Daniel said, fiercely and disbelievingly.

"You have no idea what you are facing!" Amaeron snarled.

"Can I ask why I should?" Daniel asked, trying to be rude in order to break Amaeron's pride.

This was too much for Amaeron. He gave an earth-shaking roar at Daniel.

"And they wonder why tigers cannot be provoked." Daniel said, sarcastically.

"You want to learn the hard way, fine." Amaeron snarled. "But mark my words; you will live to regret it!"

And with that, Amaeron faded into darkness and Daniel looked around to find himself back in the mansion with

John staring at him. Alfred and Angel ran up the stairs leading to the parlor.

"Don't ever leave us like that again." Alfred said, even though he was grinning.

"You've forgotten this." Angel said as she handed Daniel his T-shirt. He quickly wore it.

"What did Amaeron say?" John asked.

"He was scared of Chrumesteeler." Daniel laughed.

"And why are you laughing?" John said scornfully.

"Because I finally hear him admit that there was someone stronger than him."

"Can you concentrate and start preparing to stop this threat?"

"Now you're talking."

Once again, the giant Tigerton was about to start a whole new adventure.

"See you in a flash." Tiger Fist growled and at light speed, he ran to the country of Aeachoria.

Chapter 4

The Mighty Army ... and a Hero's Defeat

An army of one million soldiers stood before the Aeachorian fortress. At the top of the highest tower, Chrumesteeler along with his son; Chrumesteeler Jr. looked at the eager men.

"Dying is not an option!" The deep voice of Chrumesteeler echoed. "Today we will remind the world who was her master! We will show the fools of England the power of the Chorians!"

"May the king live forever!" Zaphuna shouted.

"LONG LIVE THE KING!" The army boomed.

"Father, what's that?" Chrumesteeler Jr. asked.

In the barren desert of Aeachoria, a Tigerton figure was seen. It was Tiger Fist. He gave a roar that made the army tremble. Chrumesteeler looked in disbelief.

"It's Amaeron. He's still alive!" The tyrant snapped. "Get him out of our way!"

"Aeachorian Attackers, fire at the intruder!" Morlan demanded.

The giant tanks shot electricity from their cannons at Tiger Fist. With a grin, Tiger Fist evaded these blasts with a stylish, quick dodge. He ran at supersonic speed and rammed three 'Aeachorian Attackers', destroying them. This made Chrumesteeler's helmet to fume.

Tiger Fist sent the soldiers flying with a 'Tiger Tornado' move. He evaded all the attacks and blasts that came from the weapons.

Technology has really improved in this country.' Tiger Fist thought, even while taking out hundreds of the Aeachorian soldiers.

Unable to risk any losses if this continued, Chrumesteeler jumped from the tall tower, shaking the ground and sending Tiger Fist and the soldiers off balance. Tiger Fist gave an astonishing stare at Chrumesteeler. He was over ten feet tall and every part of his body was covered with armour.

"So you must be Chrumesteeler." Tiger Fist growled, and began walking like a real tiger.

"So this is your way of revenge, Amaeron" Chrumesteeler said, but paused when Tiger Fist shook his head.

"Why does every enemy think I am Amaeron?!" Tiger Fist spluttered. "I am Tiger Fist; Amaeron's half son."

"That's a childish name." Chrumesteeler scoffed. "I reckon you are a child with the powers of a Tigerton."

"Reckon *this* for childish act!" Tiger Fist snarled.

He gave a powerful jab to the core of Chrumesteeler's

stomach. Nothing happened. Chrumesteeler gave a deep chuckle.

"That *was* a childish act!" The armoured king grinned. He threw a punch at Tiger Fist.

The punch was easy for a Tigerton to evade. He then did a 'Tigerton Flurry' move by which Tiger Fist delivered powerful combos of punches, scratches and kicks.

To his dreadful surprise, it didn't haze the ten foot Chrumesteeler.

"H-How is this possible?" Tiger Fist asked.

"Nothing's impossible for me" Chrumesteeler said.

"One, that question didn't want an answer and two, that is my motto!" Tiger Fist snarled, as he lunged at Chrumesteeler at the speed of light.

Chrumesteeler found it difficult to use his new weapons because of how fast Tiger Fist was moving. Most of the soldiers interrupted the fight but Tiger Fist easily took them out.

"Stand still, feline!" A frustrated Chrumesteeler shouted.

"Sorry, I don't do the statue." Tiger Fist said, cheekily. "But you are too slow!"

In a show of anger, Chrumesteeler shot a ball of plasma from his U.B.P.G.C. Tiger Fist repelled the ball of plasma back to Chrumesteeler, causing an explosion. As the dust cleared, Chrumesteeler was found struggling to stand.

"Not so invincible now, are you?" Tiger Fist teased.

"That was just a tickle." Chrumesteeler chuckled.

"Well then, prepare to die laughing."

Tiger Fist let out a loud roar. The roar produced sound waves strong enough to send the Aeachorian soldiers and

Chrumesteeler flying in the air. After the roar died down, they fell with a thud.

"Now that's something to laugh about." Tiger Fist laughed, falling down in the sequence.

This was too much for Chrumesteeler Jr. to handle. He took his heavy sword and rushed to Tiger Fist.

"And now, Junior comes out on the field." Tiger Fist teased. Chrumesteeler Jr. was about four inches taller than him.

Junior ignored him and rushed at him. Tiger Fist kept evading with style and ease, mocking Junior. He then countered with a slap of his paw.

"Horuun, enhance my strength and speed!" Chrumesteeler commanded.

With magical dust from his container, Horuun shouted some enchanting words. With the words said, Chrumesteeler realized he could run and fight at supersonic speed.

Tiger Fist easily outmatched Junior in every way. As he was about to send junior flying around, something very hard, and fast hit him.

Tiger Fist quickly got up. "What the heck was that?"

Suddenly in a whoosh, Chrumesteeler rushed in front of Tiger Fist and gave a powerful thrash. Tiger Fist struggled to his feet.

"Who is the slow one now?" Chrumesteeler asked.

Tiger Fist then used his 'Tiger sense' technique that slows down time. He quickly spotted Chrumesteeler running straight to him. He quickly evaded him. Concentrating, Tiger Fist countered Chrumesteeler's next attack with a 'Tiger Flurry' move. Once again, his strength was proven useless to Chrumesteeler's armour.

"What is your armour made of, Invincium?" Tiger Fist asked, angrily.

"That's a catchy name for a collection of all transition metals." Chrumesteeler said, surprisingly.

He gave a lightning-quick hook punch to the jaw of Tiger Fist, sending him into the ground. He gave up and shrugs off the pain.

"Since when did you move so fast?" Tiger Fist asked, swelling up in anger.

"Magic is always the answer to the impossible." Chrumesteeler smirked.

Tiger Fist produced four blades of wind in a scratch-like motion. The blades of wind struck Chrumesteeler, sending him flat to the ground. As he quickly got up, both he and Tiger Fist. As he quickly got up, both he and Tiger Fist realized that there were claw-like marks across his chest plate.

Tiger Fist gave a sly grin. He quickly used the move dozens of times but Chrumesteeler dodged the attacks, thanks to his newly found speed.

Chrumesteeler and Tiger Fist ran towards each other at blinding speed. With all his might, Chrumesteeler punched Tiger Fist, sending him flying out of sight. The soldiers cheered with triumph. Chrumesteeler then ordered the ambush to be postponed.

"Horuun, create more of this 'invincium' metal." Chrumesteeler ordered.

"That is a very difficult undertaking, but it shall be ready in six days."

"Aaron, improve on those weapons." Zaphuna ordered.

Chapter 5

The Great Training

Daniel woke up to find himself lying in a dark alley of London. He was wearing a large pair of shorts and the jet boosters. Before anyone could see him, he ran faster than the speed of sound by which he headed back to Los Angeles.

"How did it go?" Angel asked, hugging Daniel as he entered the house.

"Did you show them who the big cat is?" Alfred asked.

"Well… he's a little tougher than I thought." Daniel admitted.

"What really happened?" John asked.

Daniel quickly told them about Chrumesteeler and his 'invincible' armour.

"What metal is his suit made of?" John asked, reading a large chemistry book.

"I don't know." Daniel said as his sores and bruises healed. "It could be a large combination of transition metals."

"Well, check out what the internet says about Chrome stealing." Alfred said who was all the time browsing on Daniel's laptop. Everyone rushed to the laptop.

"It shows that Chrome staller"

"It's Chrumesteeler." Daniel said, irritatingly.

"His real name is Daien Arcrealto." John said.

"I never knew it was possible to be born with Herculean strength." Alfred admitted.

"The only reason why that armour-face is tough is because of his twisted wizard, Horuun." Daniel scoffed, unhappy about his loss.

"It is said Horuun was the one who created his suit of armour through sorcery" Angel read.

"That would explain why the suit is nearly invulnerable." Daniel said, although he wasn't surprised.

"What do you mean 'nearly'?" John asked. "Nothing could even cause a scratch on his armour."

"Well, I can." Daniel said. "It seems I need to be angry to be strong enough to pierce his armour."

"Have you forgotten the last time you got angry?" Alfred asked in a panic stricken voice.

Daniel remembered. He sent an abandoned truck into space, out of the earth's orbit in a rage.

"Did you know that Chrumesteeler is over three hundred years of age?" Alfred shuddered. "Is it even humanly possible?"

Angel replied. "No, but what if someone who lived in the past did something so bad to Chrumesteeler that he wants revenge?"

"Well, he did mistake me for Amaeron." Daniel said,

taking a bite of a turkey leg. "I wonder what rivalry did they both have in the past."

Alfred sighed. "Hello, that's why the internet is here. Chrumesteeler made a rivalry with King Henry of England when he betrayed him in a bloody war in the 1800s."

"What of Amaeron?"

"Man, enough of the meat. Eat chocolate for a change!"

"How conscientious, Alfred. Well, what're we gonna do?"

"Why don't you train us to help fight with you?" Angel said, suddenly.

"That's a good idea." Alfred said. For a moment, he imagined himself fighting thugs alongside Tiger Fist, and the damsels in distress he would be saving.

Daniel and John looked at each other for a moment and they both started to laugh.

"Can I please laugh at what is funny?" Alfred asked, sarcastically.

"Let's just say, for you to do my work out is unbearable." Daniel gasped for air.

"Can you still teach us the fighting techniques?" Angel asked.

"Angel, it will be too dangerous for you two when I fight Chrumesteeler." Daniel said to Angel, hoping to reassure her, and Alfred.

Alfred sighed. "Fine, we wouldn't help you with your fight against Chrumesteeler, but at least teach us your techniques."

Daniel said. "Alright, hopefully I will also benefit from training you." Daniel said. He had never actually 'train' anyone in his new methods of fighting.

"You'd better start training now!" John ordered.

Without a second thought, Daniel transformed into Tiger Fist. "Let's get started."

With the help of John, Tiger Fist extended the basement for training.

Tiger Fist started training Angel and Alfred his technique. For a moment, it was like teaching penguins how to fly. And soon, they quickly started to learn. Alfred spent hours punching a punching bag with boxing gloves. Angel practiced her punches and kicks that Tiger Fist taught her. As for Tiger Fist, he started to train for his next confrontation with Chrumesteeler.

Meanwhile in Aeachoria, soldiers practiced their combat fighting techniques. Chrumesteeler practiced to improve his strength, speed and agility. Chrumesteeler went through some brutal training with Zaphuna.

Horuun was, by now, very busy collecting and combining some essences needed for the 'invincium' metal. He was assisted by his granddaughter. Anna was a teenage prodigy in sorcery. Every day, she practiced a certain spell.

Aaron started carrying out experiments on the new and improved plasma shooting tanks and weapons. Other scientists assisted in the reactions of alloys.

Chapter 6

Odd Happenings

Autumn rushed by quickly and soon school started. Under a strict warning, Alfred said nothing about Daniel's alter ego. Daniel had a frustrated and hectic day at school.

There was a new student named Daien Dickson Jr. His first name drove Daniel, Alfred and Angel into suspicion. Daien was about the exact height of Chrumesteeler Jr. under cover trying to get information about Tiger Fist or was the first name just a coincidence?

"I'm not taking any chances." Daniel said. "Alfred, did you find any info about this guy?"

Alfred answered. "Yep, Daien Dickson Jr. is an Aeachorian citizen who escaped the war about to start between England, and Aeachoria."

Daniel held back his laugh. "That is the worst undercover note. No one escaped whatsoever."

"How do you even know that?" Angel asked, almost giving in to the information.

"I checked the computer in the library. Apparently, one is on the hunt for Tiger Fist."

Alfred nudged them. "Quiet, he's coming."

And with a hidden smile, they looked at the approaching Daien.

"Hallo, you must be Daniel Washington."

Daniel shook his hand. "What seems to be the case?"

"I was told you're a great Tiger Fist fan." Daien replied, his scowl turning to a grin.

Daniel and Angel hid their astonishment. Where the heck did Daien get that information from?

"Well... I hope I get to see him in the flesh." Daniel really wished he hadn't paused for a thought.

"I did and we both have a... never mind." Daien looked at Angel. Her blond hair eyes attracted him. "And you must be Angel Keller."

Angel gave a faint smile, although not making eye contact.

"It is said you were kidnapped by a Tigerton. Where were your friends, then?"

Daniel felt his eye twitch. Daien was trying to set a trap here. It seems he knew about him being Tiger Fist's alter ego, but he wants to be sure of it.

"Well, they did try to call the police." Angel said, putting her hands on both Daniel and Alfred.

Daien gave a frightful grin at Daniel. "Oh, well. Thank you for your grand unveiling."

As he left, Daniel clenched his fists. Angel placed her arm around his.

"He knows, without doubt." Daniel said, through gritted teeth.

"How did he know about you in one day?" Angel asked.

With a second thought, Daniel glared at Alfred. He was sweaty and nervous. Before, he could make a run for it; Daniel grabbed him by the collar.

"You told him?! How could you?!"

Alfred confessed. "He tortured me! He squeezed it out of me!"

Angel felt sorry for Alfred. "Define 'tortured'."

"He strangled me like a rat."

"We are in big trouble!" Daniel snarled while taking a bite of a drumstick. He'd go home after school and hoped to explain things to John.

"That's true." John sighed, brushing his mustache with his finger.

"Amaeron has a lot of explaining to do." Daniel groaned, giving another bite of a drumstick. "I know he is just going to say 'I told you so'."

"I TOLD YOU SO!" Amaeron boomed, as everything went dark and he appeared.

"Did you really have to say nothing about Chrumesteeler having invulnerability and super strength?" Daniel scoffed.

Amaeron didn't listen. He was too busy snickering. It seemed like hours since he laughed. However, Daniel wasn't going to let Amaeron get the better of him... and laugh up his stripes.

"Did you even hear me the first time?" Daniel spluttered, transforming into Tiger Fist.

"Didn't I warn you about Chrumesteeler? And what did you do? You mocked me!"

"You made him sound like a weakling human. And what's more, he knows you more than I expected!"

"Whom did you get your powers from?"

"From an arrogant Tigerton who wouldn't tell me why he is so afraid of a brute of a human."

Amaeron let out a deep sigh. "Daien was my best friend, like you and that no-defense nelly of a brat."

"Alfred's got more nerves than any kid I know." Daniel protested.

"Don't count on it." Amaeron snarled. "Chrumesteeler had those traits… until the day he was betrayed by King Henry in the 1800s.

"No wonder he's after England." Daniel said.

"Chrumesteeler went mad with rage. He then turned on me when I was getting old and weak."

"So he caused your death?"

"No, he didn't kill me. My death took place moments after the hybridization of you."

"Could you pierce the armour?"

"No, the armour was enchanted by a powerful sorcerer a long time ago, just before Chrumesteeler himself was born."

"I never knew Horuun lived that long."

"So, he is still alive."

"Yeah, so now I'm dealing with Immortals."

"Immortality is not invulnerability. The only way you can pierce his armour is to be angry."

"But Tiger Fist is deranged when aggressive."

"Sometimes aggressive is perfective. Don't be afraid of becoming a monster."

"How comforting, yet I still wonder why I'm still worried." Daniel said, sarcastically.

"I have given you your answer." Amaeron faded to the darkness.

"These are not the drawings you're looking for." Alfred said in a monotone voice, waving his hand across Daniel's face.

Daniel blinked. "What was I doing?"

"You were drooling on the carpet. You should have seen your face."

"What did Amaeron say?" John asked.

"He told me how to beat Chrumesteeler." Daniel had a worried expression on his face.

"How do you do that?" Alfred asked

"In order to beat him, I must be angry." Daniel said with a scowl.

John groaned as he flopped down on his favorite armchair.

"Why are you scowling?" Alfred asked who had never seen or faced the wrath of Tiger Fist.

"When Tiger Fist is to be very angry, his strength and invulnerability grows to an unreachable height." Daniel explained. "But ... so does his obsession to spill blood."

"Oh, that's an invincible hero you have."

"There has to be another way." John said, unhappily.

"There is a way; die trying." Alfred laughed.

Daniel misunderstood the joke. "If it sounds so easy, why don't you do the second option?"

"Hey, I'm not a hero here." Alfred said cheekily.

"Anyway, we both better start training." Daniel grinned, showing his canines that were growing in length.

"Just remember never to smile." Alfred teased, slightly terrified of the canines glittering at him.

Alfred continued to learn the basics of karate along with Tiger Fist. To Tiger Fist's eyes, Alfred was very promising, and determined.

"By the time, you've learnt this techniques, I will give a brief demonstration of my 'tiger fist' moves." Tiger Fist said, lifting a one ton weight.

"I really wish I was as strong as you." Alfred said admiring the hulking strength of Tiger Fist.

"What would you do with it?" Tiger Fist asked.

"I would throw a truck at any one who dares to tick me off."

Meanwhile in Aeachoria, Horuun and Anna watched the conversation through a magic fountain.

"Do you sense it, Anna?" Horuun asked who seemed completely astonished.

"Even Tiger Fist has a few friends that seem weak."

"Don't see, my child. Feel the power surging through that young mortal."

Anna gasped. "Isn't that?"

"Yes, that boy is the reincarnation of Taurus, god of strength."

"Does she even know?" Anna asked. She never found interest in boys. Why is she still staring at Alfred?

"Since that Taurus refuses to descend completely on the mortal, he has no idea what he is capable of."

"So what do we do now?" Anna asked, solemnly.

"Let us give him a boost of hatred in his system." Horuun smirked.

With a wave of his hands, the sorcerer cast an enchantment on Alfred. Back at the mansion, Alfred started to groan in pain.

"Alfred, what's happening?" Tiger Fist asked as he carried Alfred to the living room.

"The pain ... it's too much." Alfred wheezed as his eyes turned watery, and red.

John took a container labeled Tylenol. "Take two of these."

Alfred gulped the medicine with water. "Ugh, those taste bitter!"

"Well, at least it is better than chewing vegetables." Tiger Fist said, taking a bite of a chicken leg. Alfred looked at him.

"Couldn't you eat something that doesn't have blood?" He teased but shuddered when Tiger Fist grinned.

Tiger Fist quickly finished the leg and transformed back into Daniel. Daniel noticed Alfred's eyes watery red.

"Are you okay?" He asked.

"What does it look like?" Alfred asked, suddenly hard hearted.

"It is just that your eyes are red." Daniel said, slightly surprised at his friend's anger.

"It's just because I didn't get enough sleep." Alfred claimed. "I'm going home."

"You're not waiting for your father?" John asked.

"He will understand." Alfred answered, still frowning. He took his bag and left.

"What's wrong with him?" John asked.

"It must be the training stress." Daniel snickered, going back to his training.

"Are you ever going to take a break?" John asked, sipping some hot cocoa.

"I'm still not tired." That was all Daniel could say.

Outside his house, Alfred staggered to the front porch. He looked at his skin. His tan color turned red. He soon realized that his vision made everything he saw red.

"What's happening to me?" Alfred asked himself. Soon his father, Arnold King came rushing towards him.

"What is it, my son?" He asked.

"My eyes… they're burning!" Alfred groaned.

Arnold looked into Alfred's eyes in horror. "No, this cannot be happening now!"

Alfred felt a rage in him. Arnold helped him into the house.

"Try to relax, Alfred." Arnold said as he laid Alfred on the mat and wore a traditional necklace with a bull-like head carved on the end of it.

He then did a prayer. Alfred wanted to ask his father what he was doing, but the pain held him back.

"TAURUS IS RAISED!" Alfred bellowed in a voice that wasn't his.

"No, I was too late!" Arnold cried, taking steps backwards.

Alfred's memory was completely engulfed and he gave a grin. He began to grow red fur from his body. Bull horns pierced from his head. He then began to have a face of a bull and a tail grew. Arnold felt like fainting as he saw his son.

"He lives again." He muttered. He had failed to have trained his son better. Now, the curse of Taurus has been unleashed to destroy anything he sees. "Alfred, try and overcome the curse!"

"I am not Alfred." The minotaur-like creature bellowed. "I am Taurus, the Aeachorian god of strength!"

He then grabbed Arnold and kept hitting him against the walls. He later threw him out of the house. Not very far away, Daniel sensed the sudden, horrific monster at Alfred's house.

"What is it?" John asked, as he saw Daniel's horrified face.

"Something has gone very wrong." Daniel said. "AWAKEN THE TIGER FIST."

Soon the tall, muscular Tigerton ran at super speed to Alfred's house. He spotted Arnold, moaning in pain.

Chapter 8

Best of Friends

"Run! Alfred… is Taurus." Arnold gasped.

"I will get you to a hospital." The deep voice of Tiger Fist said.

"Without me showing you true power, Daniel?!" Taurus (Alfred) appeared, crashing the house down.

"Alfred? What happened to you?"

"It's Taurus now!" The minotaur-like monster bellowed. "My strength will easily outmatch yours."

"I will not fight you, Alfred. You are my best friend."

"Didn't I tell you my name is Taurus?" Taurus snarled, exhaling deeply from his nostrils, like a real bull. He skidded with one foot.

"Tell it to someone who cares. Your father is going to die if he doesn't go to the hospital."

"Save *that* for someone who cares. By now, I had informed Chrumesteeler about Angel and he had issued orders for her kidnapping."

"You told him about her? How could you?"

"I did it through the power of the wizard, Horuun. I am

the god of strength. What? Never been betrayed before?"

At accurately the speed of light, Tiger Fist picked up Arnold, took him to a nearby hospital and returned to his spot, glaring at Taurus. Taurus blinked. All this happened under a quick blink of Taurus.

"What? Whatever." Taurus hesitated.

An enraged Tiger Fist zoomed at Taurus in a flash, crashing them both into Alfred's house. Even though Taurus was as strong as Tiger Fist, he was outmatched by Tiger Fist's speed. Tiger Fist then roared and produced powerful sound waves at Taurus, sending him flying in the air. Taurus quickly recovered and lowered his horns like a bull. With a bull's bellow, he lunged at Tiger Fist at a speed rate faster than a normal human. Tiger Fist easily evaded the rush, causing Taurus to crash into a nearby building. Tiger Fist grabbed Taurus and swung him round in a circle before releasing him.

Taurus was flung from L.A to New York. Tiger Fist was close behind him with his speed. The brawl continued with Tiger Fist having a clear upper hand of it. Tiger Fist growled and he raised his hands horizontally whilst spinning wildly into a tornado, sucking Taurus before he made a move.

Tiger Fist did a 'Velocity Claw Slash', by which in a mighty motion-like scratch, he made three claw-like blades of wind that gave Taurus a claw mark. The weakened Taurus collapsed on a nearby Benz, crushing it under his weight. Tiger Fist swiftly grabbed Taurus by the neck and started to choke him.

"Daniel, I am your friend." Taurus wheezed as he slowly changed back into Alfred.

Tiger Fist didn't buy it. Alfred had betrayed him one time too many. He squeezed him tighter. In Aeachoria, the imprisoned Angel tearfully watched the fight along with Chrumesteeler, Junior, Horuun and Anna through a large magical mirror. Anna did seem to be as horrified as Angel.

"Does the fighting bother you, sorceress?" Chrumesteeler Jr. asked with a chuckle.

"I lack the courage to see bloodshed, Your Majesty." Anna answered.

"Why are you doing this?" Angel asked shaking the chains bounded on her hands.

"I don't tolerate unwanted nuisances to ambush me and live." Chrumesteeler replied, coldly.

Anna then left the throne room. She whispered an incantation to herself.

Tiger Fist held up a fist to finish Taurus, who had now changed from his minotaur-like state to Alfred.

"I am your best friend." Alfred wheezed, tears gushing from his eyes.

Suddenly, Tiger Fist received a flashback of his old monk father. He remembered how he drove the old monk to his death in his rage. He also remembered Alfred's friendship with him. He quickly released his grip. Alfred miraculously recovered. He stared at Tiger Fist.

"Forgive me, my friend." Tiger Fist muttered.

"You remembered our friendship. That is what really matters." Alfred replied.

"I have to go to Aeachoria, but I will take you to your father first."

Tiger Fist took Alfred to the Ajax hospital where Arnold was lying in an emergency room. Arnold was fading fast.

As Tiger Fist left for Aeachoria, Alfred turned to Arnold.

"Forgive me, Father." Alfred said, tears dripping from his eyes. "I have killed you."

"You... didn't... kill... me." Arnold gasped. "Taurus did this."

"If I was a better son to you, none of this would have happened." Alfred said.

"No... it is my fault. I should have told you."

"Daniel has gone to free Angel. There is no way he can do it by himself."

"Go... and assist him."

"But I cannot control Taurus' tension. He is not like Tiger Fist."

"There is a way. I will show you."

Chapter 9

Against the Aeachoria Army

Tiger Fist ran as fast as he could, fast enough to run across the ocean without sinking. It took him an hour and a half to reach the great walls of Aeachoria. With a push, he made the walls collapse. From a great distance, he saw the Aeachorian army. There could be more than thirty thousand soldiers. They all wore the armour similar to Chrumesteeler's own. There were seventy of the 'Aeachorian Attackers' Tanks.

'Just one of those tanks could erase an entire country.' Tiger Fist thought.

He could just run fast enough to pass them without a living thing noticing but he could not just leave armies and tanks, about to go to war.

With a powerful roar, Tiger Fist jumped to the battlefield. He completely caught the soldiers off guard as he lifted the barrel of an 'Aeachorian Attacker' and used it to bash any soldier in sight. Before Zaphuna caught up with the situation, Tiger Fist had dismantled four thousand Aeachorian soldiers.

"He has become stronger!" Morlan warned. "Swordsmen, attack!"

It didn't take Tiger Fist a minute to give the swordsmen a run for their lives.

"Those were my finest men." Morlan grumbled, picking up his U.B.P.G.C. "This feline is really ticking me off!"

"Tick this!" Tiger Fist shouted as he threw a tank at Morlan and Zaphuna.

Zaphuna was quick to evade the attack, but Morlan was crushed by the tank. Enraged, he picked his U.B.P.G.C and started aiming at Tiger Fist. Tiger Fist was too fast for Zaphuna and the soldiers to even see.

In a whoosh of wind, Tiger Fist crippled Zaphuna with a paralyzing finger jab to the neck. He then gave a 'Supersonic Roar' and not only did he produce supersonic waves with his voice, but also started to weaken the weather fabric of the entire continent. This move dismantled the rest of the soldiers. The four thousand men who were left retreated. Tiger Fist continued to the giant fortress.

"He's coming here?!" Chrumesteeler ranted, when the news reached the fortress. "What happened to my army?"

"He defeated them." One of the surviving soldiers answered. "He has become stronger than our last encounter."

"You TOLD me that the metals were unbreakable!" Chrumesteeler Jr. shouted.

"I didn't expect a creature to be that strong." Horuun said. "These metals are the hardest known to man."

Aaron laughed. "Let him come. You didn't think I would help build your fortress unprotected, did you?"

"You did it with the help of magic." Horuun said, irritatingly.

Tiger Fist tried to push the door open, but jumped back when he experienced some electric sparks.

'*Interesting, looks like I need to be angry to pull this off.*'
He began to push the door again, grunting and groaning as he felt the electricity shocking him. As he got angrier, he started to grow in height and muscles. Soon he destroyed the door with ease. At the speed faster than the human eye, Tiger Fist rushed through the secured halls of the fortress without triggering a trap.

"Horuun, divert Tiger Fist or keep him busy!" Chrumesteeler ordered.

As Tiger Fist was about to burst into the throne room, a giant trapdoor opened underneath him. The palace guards and soldiers went in after him.

The giant trapdoor led to a giant cave. Tiger Fist easily defeated the guards and soldiers. Just when he was about to go further, giant trolls and orcs appeared from the darkness of the cave. Tiger Fist suddenly went berserk and his strength and invulnerability began skyrocketing.

Tiger Fist transformed into a gigantic and muscular Tigerton monster. His orange fur turned red. He was over thirteen feet tall.

"What is that?" Chrumesteeler asked, looking in horror. "He's become bigger than me."

Tiger Fist swung his three foot long tail and gave a tremendous roar.

"TIGER FIST IS ANGRY!" The giant Tigerton monster boomed. "TIGER FIST NOW IS ANGRY FIST!"

"Angry Fist, that's what he comes up with?" Chrumesteeler Jr. laughed to himself.

The trolls and orcs charged at Angry Fist (Tiger Fist). With an insane use of his new power, Angry Fist created havoc out of the trolls and orcs. Within minutes, Angry Fist broke through the cave.

He crashed into the throne room, finding Chrumesteeler, Junior, Horuun, Anna and Angel looking as calm as possible.

"It was so nice of you to drop in." Chrumesteeler said, ironically.

"Save the villain speech for someone who cares!" Angry Fist snarled. He gave a low growl that made Horuun shake.

"Hang on! This place is too tight for a battle." Chrumesteeler reassured.

Horuun quickly understood and teleported everyone in the throne room to a deserted battlefield.

"That's better!" Chrumesteeler Jr. exclaimed.

"Allow us to deal with him, sire." Horuun pleaded, as he and Anna walked towards Angry Fist.

They both shouted a powerful spell and Angry Fist was bounded in chains.

"Don't bother trying to break through." Horuun boasted. "These chains are indestructibly-"

Before he could even finish the sentence, Angry Fist broke through the chains, like paper.

"Lost your tongue, wizard?" Aaron asked, trying hard not to laugh.

Enraged, Horuun summoned large meteors from space to crash on Angry Fist. This caused a mighty earthquake that shook every fragment of the earth. An explosion occurred next.

Horuun smirked as the black dust of smoke rose, but became horrified to find Angry Fist standing, without even a bruise.

Horuun stuttered as he stumbled to the ground in his shocked state.

"All you did was made me angry!" Angry Fist roared and with a paw swipe, he crippled Horuun.

"That's so much for relying on magic." Aaron murmured.

"Why don't I even the odds?" A loud, deep voice suggested.

"Who spoke just now?" Chrumesteeler asked.

Out of the smoke came a bigger and stronger Taurus. Angry Fist looked astonished.

"I knew that this day could get a lot worse." Junior grumbled.

Chapter 10

The Final Battle

"Release Angel or prepare to lose your throne!" Angry Fist ordered.

"Have you forgotten that you couldn't even cause a dent on my armour?" Chrumesteeler asked, arrogantly.

This made Angry Fist bare his claws and Taurus lower his horns.

"You are not the only one who has changed." Chrumesteeler Jr. said and he lifted his sword, and rushed at Taurus.

Angry Fist gave a roar and lunged at Chrumesteeler. The armoured king found himself outmatched by the monstrous Angry Fist, widely in strength. Adding to Chrumesteeler's horror is that Angry Fist's strength was powerful enough to tear his armour apart.

Meanwhile Chrumesteeler Jr. and Taurus were having a gruesome battle of their own. With his newly found strength and being able to control himself, Taurus was able to take on Chrumesteeler Jr.

In the heat of battle, Taurus exhaled furiously. Instead of carbon dioxide, he exhaled carbon monoxide smoke that clouded him and Chrumesteeler Jr. This gave him the chance to 'bull charge' Jr. into a nearby hill.

Angry Fist held a weak and worn out Chrumesteeler by the neck.

"You are finished, metal freak!" Angry Fist said, and he started squeezing the throat of Chrumesteeler.

Suddenly, Angry Fist transformed into Tiger Fist again. This shocked him and released Chrumesteeler. The armoured king wheezed as he tried to get his breath. He then looked at Tiger Fist and smirked.

"You are useless in this form." Chrumesteeler said in a show of arrogance.
    "Really, I didn't get that memo. Hit me!" Tiger Fist grinned.
    Chrumesteeler soon realized how fast Tiger Fist was. "It doesn't matter. You will eventually get tired and I'll"

Before he noticed Tiger Fist's new-found temper, he tried to shoot him with his ultra-barreled plasma gun. At lightning speed, Tiger Fist swiped the weapon out of Chrumesteeler's hand with his paw. Chrumesteeler managed to aim a well-placed blow at the distracted Tigerton.

"You have proven to be a challenge for Aeachoria." Chrumesteeler laughed. "We are all going to miss you."

Staring at the weeping Angel, Tiger Fist's eyes were filled with rage. He got up and delivered a 'Claw Frenzy Barrage', powerful swipes of the claws, at Chrumesteeler.

The power emitted from the paws was strong enough to destroy Chrumesteeler's armoured chest plate.

For the first time in hundreds of years, Chrumesteeler could see the pale white of his skin. Before he could even react to his shocking experience, Tiger Fist grew and transformed once again to the nearly invulnerable Angry Fist.

In a heartbeat, Angry Fist destroyed Chrumesteeler's armour and crippled the armoured king. Stunned, Chrumesteeler felt his face.

Taurus was about to finish off Chrumesteeler Jr., but froze as he caught sight of Chrumesteeler's face. Junior also looked in shock. This was because he didn't look like his father.

Angry Fist broke Angel's chains, freeing her and he used the chains to strangle Chrumesteeler.

"NO, STOP IT!" Angel shrieked. Angry Fist loosened his grip, and looked at Angel.

A recovering Horuun looked up at the scene. Realizing what he nearly did, Angry Fist released an unconscious Chrumesteeler. Becoming completely calm, he transformed back into Tiger Fist. Angel began to pet the fur of Tiger Fist's arm.

"Stop doing that." Tiger Fist grinned.

Anna helped Chrumesteeler Jr. to his feet before Taurus noticed. When he did, he stared at the beautiful sorceress.

"I plead for you to cease this fight." Anna said. "You've won."

Chapter 11

What's next?

"This wouldn't have happened if you and your 'king' had left us." Taurus said.

"What my king wishes is my command." Anna answered.

"Doesn't it bother you to be trapped in his grasp and using your powers at his command?"

Anna hesitated. "Please do not deceive me, Taurus."

"Was it you who did this to me?"

"Yes, under my master's wishes. I'm sorry."

"Well, it wasn't your fault. I forgive you."

Anna looked surprisingly at Taurus. No one had forgiven her of a chaos like this.

"Come with us." Taurus offered. "You don't need this life of imprisonment."

"The law of Aeachoria forbids me to join you. Thank you, anyway."

As she left, Taurus jumped back to find Tiger Fist, who had probably heard the whole situation.

"A minotaur and a witch don't quite mix." Tiger Fist teased.

"Just be glad I'm in a good mood."

"Speaking of that, how did you control yourself?" Tiger Fist asked.

"Dad gave me this charm, which I had to swallow in order to gain control of the monster in me."

"Does he know about Taurus?"

"Taurus placed a curse on my ancestor centuries ago. He is the Aeachorian god of strength."

"Let's go home and get a rest." Angel said, quickly.

"Does it take you kids so long to beat those armoured goons?" John asked who was waiting for them in his private jet.

"What made you think we would return?" Tiger Fist asked.

"I didn't think; I knew." John said as they all entered the plane and left.

Once recovered, Chrumesteeler went into a rage. "We will meet again, Tiger Fist. And you will regret that you ever crossed me."

"Don't forget he has a twin brother." A Tigerton said who seemed familiar. And that Tigerton was Dabiasto.

THE END